Dear Reader,

Michael's, Inc., was a computer company in Indianapolis that had genius inventors who couldn't be lured away. So we bought the company. The head of personnel was the worst of the tolerated deadwood. His secretary was a mind-stunning woman named Sarah Moore, and she was the most efficient of all of the Michael's, Inc., staff. I knew immediately that no other man had the discipline to be normal around Miss Moore, so I volunteered to be responsible for her in the takeover. It was the only thing to do. The really irritating part of it was that she didn't consider me a *possible*.

Steven Blake

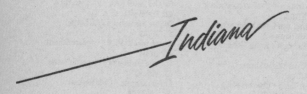

D0424142

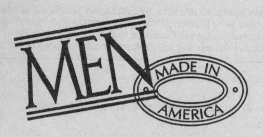

LASS SMALL

Possibles

Indiana

Published by Silhouette Books New York

America's Publisher of Contemporary Romance

To my sister Marian Gittinger Anderson

SILHOUETTE BOOKS
300 East 42nd St., New York, N.Y. 10017

POSSIBLES

Copyright © 1987 by Lass Small

ISBN: 0-373-45164-4

Published Silhouette Books 1987, 1993

Printed in the U.S.A.

One

———

Sarah Moore was a woman with no pretenses. A little above average height, she was nicely rounded, long legged and redheaded. She had sparkling blue eyes that appeared at times to glint with lightning. Her short nose missed being called "pug," and her small mouth had a full lower lip, that could look either very sensual or quite stubborn. She wasn't aware of the "sensual," but she struggled with the "stubborn."

It was the third Tuesday in April, in Indianapolis, and Sarah was late getting to Mattie's house. She rapped twice before opening the door to the muted roar of a roomful of women. Shouting "Sorry I'm late" to no one in particular, she draped her coat over the newel post.

It was the monthly meeting of the Possibles.

Across heads, Mattie gave Sarah a smile and then tapped her coffee cup with her spoon. "Okay. Okay. Hey, all you guys, be quiet. Let's get this over with." Not quite according to Robert's Rules of Order, obviously, and the resulting meeting gave ample evidence of the group's casualness.

"Any new business?"

"There's a new guy where I work who might be one."

"And you're tossing him into the basket already?" came one astonished query.

"He's too short for me, but you might like him, Mary."

Mary complained, "I get all the short ones."

"Well, you can hardly be so selfish as to want the tall ones," someone else put in.

"Just how short is he?" another inquired.

"I haven't actually measured him, but I don't think he could be more than five-five."

Mary groused, "We'd have all boys and not one would be over five feet tall."

"You don't *have* to marry him."

"I know. But short men tend to get very masterful with short women."

"They're no violets with tall women either," a sultry voice put in. "I remember..."

"Please, Libby, don't let's start on your life and loves. We haven't the time and the rest of us will just gnash our teeth in envy."

"I know." Libby gave a throaty laugh amid groans of various kinds.

"I'm returning Louis St. Ives," Sarah said from her spot in the crowd sitting on the floor. "He's a very sweet man. An excellent Possible."

"Then why are you returning him?"

"I'm just not right for him. He needs someone more tactful and gentle. You all know me. It would take an unusual man to marry me and be happy."

Damned if they all didn't agree! Somewhat disgruntled, Sarah leaned back against the chair behind her and felt grumpy. The trouble with friends was they felt perfectly comfortable being honest. She listened as they argued who would be the next to try Louis St. Ives. And it was Mattie who won! Mattie?

Sarah was so engrossed in trying to see the plausibility of a match between Mattie and Louis that she didn't keep track of the exchange and was surprised when Mattie called out, "Sarah!" and it was apparent her name hadn't been spoken for the first time.

Sarah raised her brows as if she were being patient in the noisy room, so Mattie asked again, "If there're any good Possibles coming in with the takeover at Michaels Inc., be sure to spread them around."

"We'll get the rejects," was one sulky comment.

"No." Sarah rose to her knees and then stood elegantly. "I've decided to give up on men. I'll do whatever I can for you hopefuls. But I'm twenty-nine now and I find the whole struggle with Possibles is a chore. I shall leave the field to all of you." She bowed to cheers, stepped across and around the women crowded in the room, got her coat and gave a farewell wave as she exited Mattie's house.

The next day she went by to see her mother and told her the same thing: "I'm through."

Her mother placidly counted the stitches on her left knitting needle and replied, "Like hell."

"I've spent a good twelve years at this and that's more than enough time. There just isn't a man out there for me."

"Yet." Her mother went on knitting.

"I'm not like you. I don't think I'm meant to marry."

Her mother snorted.

On Thursday, the "returned" Louis St. Ives came by Sarah's apartment, which was a part of an old house in the Broad Ripple section of town. He came in the morning, before work, and impatiently rang her doorbell.

Already wearing her hat—an enveloping, cloth one—she opened the door. Seeing Louis, she took a deep breath and mentioned politely, "This is a little early," before she inquired, "Is something wrong?" She glanced significantly at his shirt-sleeves in the cool, April air.

"Sarah, you can't mean it. You have to listen to me."

"We've gone over this three times. I like you. You're a neat man. You'll make some woman a good husband. But not me. With me, you'd be miserable."

"Let me be the judge of that."

By then she was annoyed. "What you really want is sex."

"You ought to try me."

"If I were less morally structured, I'd be delighted. But it goes with the territory. I won't bed-hop. The trouble isn't in you, it's with me. You will find a woman who adores you. I'd probably not appreciate you."

"Then let's just be friends," he coaxed. "Take more time."

"I'd waste yours. You're thirty. You need to get married and have children."

"With you."

"Take my word: it would never work. Now, Louis, let's not quarrel over this. I'm really tired of going over and over the same words. Neither of us will convince the other. Someday you'll thank your stars you're not married to me. Now, goodbye. I'm not going to be late for work. You know the chaos out there with the takeover. I'm leaving. Goodbye."

"Sarah..."

"Goodbye." She closed the door, leaving him standing, hunched against the cool wind. A very nice man. Just not the one for her. She was rather depressed to be the cause of his unhappiness—however temporary that might be—but she went through her apartment, pulling on her coat, and out the back door to her car.

She'd driven two blocks when she realized Louis was following her. That took away the discomfort she felt about him and replaced it with a strong sense of indignation. Darting her car ahead, she began to drive rather recklessly and was soon sure she'd lost him. Then she saw him again.

The whole thing was dumb. He knew where she worked. There was no reason to try to lose him in traffic. But when she saw him in the rearview mirror, her competitiveness reared its head and she impatiently crowded the custom-made car ahead of her. Instead of decently getting out of her way, it turned immediately in front of her, right into Michaels Inc.'s parking lot. She was annoyed because the male driving the car was in fact being very law-abiding, though excessively slow.

She had finally jerked her own car into a spot and got out, slammed the locked door and begun to turn away. But she found she'd caught the tail of her coat in the locked door so had to fumble for her keys, unlock the door to release the stupid coat, relock the door and slam it closed again.

By then Louis had found a place over a couple of rows and was running toward her saying, "Now, Sarah, you're being unreasonable."

That made her angry. "How like you to say I'm the one who is unreasonable!" Her lower lip became stubborn and her eyes flashed like lightning. "When you point a finger at anyone, *three* of the fingers on that hand point back at *you*!"

The law-abiding male who had hampered her getting into the parking lot before Louis arrived was crossing the lot and went past two cars over. He was the biggest of the people going toward the Michaels building. Seizing the opportunity to escape Louis, Sarah called, "Here I am!" Then she snapped at Louis, "Leave me alone. Go away! Goodbye!" With that, she turned around with a swirl of her abused coat and ran toward the stranger, who had hesitated and now watched her with an expressionless face.

He instantly judged her as an attractive handful. The worst kind of woman. He noted the shirt-sleeved man who was obviously upset. And dangerous? No visible weapons. Domestic quarrel? Just what he needed. Damn!

Speaking to him in a carrying voice, so the man in shirt-sleeves could hear, the woman said in a rush, "Sorry I'm late." She took his arm and urged him forward. "I couldn't get through traffic, but we can still have half a cup." She chattered, not giving him any opportunity to object, reply or question. That was just as well, for what could he say?

He looked back twice, and he looked down at her the rest of the time. His face wasn't welcoming. She prayed he wouldn't jerk his arm free and betray her. Louis would simply *love* to "rescue" her. It could be horribly embarrassing. She hurried them along with the others who arrowed toward the entrance: her goal. After they were through the door, the stranger could do whatever he wanted.

She didn't look back, her whole attention was on getting to the door. They did get there, and the stranger opened the door and held it for her. She ducked through in relief. He took his time following, turning to look back at the lone, shirt-sleeved figure standing in the wind. Then the stranger followed Sarah inside and inquired, "Husband?"

"No. Thank you for not pushing me aside and running away. You must think I'm a blithering idiot." She removed her hat without disturbing her sleek hair, smoothly captured in a bun at the back of her head.

He watched that as he inquired, "Boyfriend?"

"Not anymore."

"Lovers' quarrel?"

"No."

He gave her a rather cool assessment. "He'll call you."

"I hope not. It's completely hopeless." She had been looking at him and was greatly pleased with what she saw. He was taller than she and quite nice looking in an unspectacular way. No woman wants a spectacular man; she'd have to fend off all the other women in the world. He was more subtle looking. Brown hair, dark eyes, shaggy brows, long eyelashes, stern mouth and a good nose. Nice, athlete's body. She smiled. "You're not one of us."

He replied immediately, "No."

She laughed. "You're lucky. No windows. We might just as well work in a cave."

"It's energy efficient."

She countered cheerfully, "It's boring." They began to move with the stream of people down the center hall, but since they were talking, or at least she was, they moved more slowly and others went around them. She continued with logic, "With no windows, how can we tell what the weather is like? Or what season it is?" She was teasing for a smile, but he wasn't smiling. "Are you planning to work here?"

"Yes."

"Really?" Her smile was wide with delight. "What division?"

"Personnel."

"Oh good! That's my section. What job?"

"Vice-president." He gave her a cool look.

"Great!" She had a nice chuckle. "I like a man with ambition. My boss, Mr. Taylor, our VP of personnel. He's an easygoing man but everything's in chaos. Michaels Inc. has been taken over by a conglomerate called Calhoun Incorporated, based in Chicago, and heads have rolled. You picked a bad time to start a new job." She stopped and looked up at him to say with friendly frankness, "I'm Mr. Taylor's secretary. If you get desperate, whistle. Maybe I can help."

He said nothing. Shy? He didn't look shy. She smiled again. "Perhaps I'll see you at lunch. We have a cafeteria. Lousy food. Maybe the new people will do something reckless about it. Good luck!" She lifted a hand in a token wave and branched off toward her own office.

He had stopped there in the hall among the flow of people reporting for work, and he watched after her quite soberly. Then he went on toward the president's office. In his mind he groused: Redheads are always trouble. This one is too. Obviously.

Michaels Inc. manufactured computer parts. What company didn't these days? It was a tidy, careful, accurate company that took pride in its products. Other than not having any outside windows, it was a good place to work.

Sarah had been there since she graduated from secretarial school, so she was quite well-informed when it came to the company and, being in personnel, she usually knew everyone and their circumstances.

The first jolt that day was the fact that Mr. Taylor had been replaced by a temporary vice-president named Steven Blake. Her contact with the new company said sardonically, "You get Old Blake." And he laughed.

Sarah asked cautiously, "What do you mean by that?"

"He's a bearcat. A stickler. You lucky girl, you. You get to be his secretary. He's unreasonable." Then he added honestly, "But fair."

"Unreasonable...but fair? How can that be?"

"If it isn't right to him, he makes it that way. Ever hear of a bear with a sore paw? That's Old Blake."

"How thrilling. You've made my day."

"You can always quit."

"That's the coward's way out."

Without her saying a word, the news went through the personnel section like wildfire. Poor Mr. Taylor had been replaced by Old Steven Blake. There were several cool heads who said replacing Taylor had been a good idea, now maybe the department could be organized more efficiently.

"More efficiently" got a good chew-over at the watercooler. And there was the usual speculation. Someone said maybe now they would get windows. That got a laugh. Then, in the middle of the morning, Sarah's business crony came along with more rumors.

Joan Parkington was a cheerful brunette. Brunettes generally smolder, but Joan didn't. She had green eyes. She would have been annoyingly good-looking, but she was married to Luke and loved him; that made her tolerable. And Luke had given her a knuckle-width wedding ring. That helped eliminate her as competition when the Possibles Club took her along as a drawing card at bars or sports events. Just her looks lured the men close enough before they saw her ring, but by then the others had a chance to smile and say hello.

So that Thursday morning, Joan leaned a hip against Sarah's desk and folded her arms over her chest as she said, "I hear you have a new boss and he'll be in this afternoon."

"Now how did you find that out so soon? I didn't even know Mr. Taylor had been canned! Here I am—his secretary—and I'm last to know!"

Joan judged, "It's because you never listen to gossip. You're too busy being efficient. Efficiency is a handicap. One must . . . communicate."

"Ah . . ." Sarah replied. "Men communicate. Women gossip."

"You got it."

"Have you seen our new Great White Father? I've heard he's old."

"I've glimpsed a raft of young, vigorous men who look like great Possibles."

"Probably all married," Sarah remarked gloomily. "All the good ones are taken."

"Well, I have Luke."

"He has one more year as an intern, right? Dr. Parkington. Sounds like a soap-opera character."

"No."

"You're a lucky, lucky woman."

Joan looked down at her fingernails and said, "Yes."

* * *

At lunch Sarah remembered to watch for the new employee to be sure that someone helped him find the cafeteria, but she didn't see him standing around looking uncertain, so he must have managed well enough. Too bad he wasn't the new VP of personnel. Old Blake. In a business as dynamic as Calhoun Incorporated, how old could Old Blake be? She looked carefully around the cafeteria but didn't see her stranger at all. Maybe he didn't stand out. Although he looked a little anonymous at first, there was a strong power to him. No one would mistake him for an ordinary man.

Perhaps he was one of the new officers connected with the takeover. But he'd quite clearly said personnel. And her informant had said "old." Interesting.

After a reasonable repair job on her makeup and a good brushing of her swinging mass of red hair before she redid the knot, Sarah returned to her office and closed the outer door. Just as she did, her buzzer sounded softly. She picked up her notebook in its folder and went into the inner office with some curiosity. She opened the door and saw him. She laughed and exclaimed, "You!"

He watched her come to him across the carpet with her open smile and her long, free stride. He stood up and extended his hand with cool courtesy. "I'm Steven Blake."

She took his hand in a firm answering grip. "How do you do? I'm Sarah Moore." She grinned then as she said, "You're much too young. I was distinctly told *Old* Mr. Blake. Is your father in the new company?"

"Even he would not be pleased to be called 'Old' Mr. Blake." He sat down behind the desk.

"Then I won't." She sat opposite him, placed her folder on his desk in front of her, opened it and turned a page sideways under her steno pad. She began to make some quick, shorthand notes as she said, "I shouldn't be surprised to find you here. You told me personnel *and* vice-president! But I didn't know then that Mr. Taylor had been replaced. What did you do with him? If you sank him in the White River, Mrs. Taylor will take a very dim view of it. She likes him.''

"He's very likable. Very inefficient. You're apparently all that kept him afloat. Don't worry about him. He has a golden parachute. Quite undeserved, in my opinion.''

Sarah's pencil hesitated in her note taking, then on the sideways paper she crossed something out. He noticed.

They took a tour of the personnel offices and she introduced him around. When they returned to his office, they were interrupted several times by key personnel who dropped by to meet the new VP. There were others who came to see if Mr. Blake had what he wanted and was comfortable. These were the bootlickers. Sarah noted them and said nothing. She soon realized Steven Blake wasn't fooled. He was courteous and not quite abrupt. More impatient. Actually, his impatience bordered on annoyance.

She made more notes on the crosswise paper.

She also met others of the takeover team who came in to consult, to request personnel, to see files on the termination of others, to shake things up. She took notes in her book and added to the fascinating side-paper tucked underneath.

She got up when the office cleared once and went out for coffee, bringing back two cups. When she came in, they were alone. Steven Blake said: "I don't know what was going on out there in the parking lot this morning, Miss Moore, but why did you choose to latch on to me?"

She smiled slightly and replied, "I knew you'd be safe."

"Safe!" He was offended.

"Most men would have assumed I was coming on to them."

"Miss Moore, that is conduct we cannot allow."

"Would you like some coffee?" she inquired formally.

"Are you ignoring my order?"

"Order?" She looked up at him as she sat down. Her voice was normal but her eyes were flashing tiny sparks.

He watched her eyes, fascinated, but his tongue went on quite clearly. "Order," he agreed to the label quite readily. "Domestic quarrels have no place in the business world."

"It was in the parking lot and it wasn't a domestic quarrel. Anyway, it's my business, not yours."

"You made it mine when you involved me."

"I didn't involve you! All I did was walk along beside you."

"Clinging to my arm. Demanding my protection."

"I did nothing of the sort!" She was flaring up and her lower lip had passed "sulky" and was becoming "stubborn."

"If he'd become violent, you would have expected me to defend you."

"Louis? Violent? Don't be ridiculous!"

"Ridiculous?" His soft deep voice was quite dangerous.

She looked at him blankly, ran through their conversation in a rapid replay and laughed!

He watched this volatile, unpredictable woman. Those expressive eyes that had been shooting anger at him were now sparkling with merriment.

With laughter tripping along her words, she said, "If I'm not fired, this will be an interesting relationship." Then she hastened to add with delicious drollery. "Employer/employee variety."

Without following her humor, he said coldly, "We will not tolerate emotional outbursts as happened this morning, Miss Moore."

She sobered slowly as she studied him. Then she said formally, "I see." She neither agreed nor disagreed. But she looked down and lined through the shorthand notes on the extra page. She did it deliberately.

Then the plant manager, Tom Cullins, came in. He had been with the company for almost four years. He was a doer. He and Steven Blake quickly found common ground and began to discuss a rough outline of job needs that were exciting to Tom. Their discussion proved Mr. Blake knew a great deal about the business and about people. Not about secretaries, but about other people.

Sarah listened and took notes—those Blake asked for and some of her own. In spite of her attention to her boss, her mind had room for speculation. She just might look for another job. This man was organized, knowledgeable, and he might be all right to work with, but if he was going to be a stiff-neck, and that critical of her, he could go jump.

She didn't need the job that badly. And now that she wasn't in the marriage market, she didn't need the contacts. She could work in an orphanage. That might fill her need for mothering. The girl-scout troop she led was great, but she would like a more expanded hand in dealing with kids.

However, when she thought about it, how many orphanages existed these days? Not very many. She could work with the learning disabled. Tutor...

"Miss Moore, could Tom have some coffee?"

Old Blake called her "Miss Moore," but he called Tom Cullins "Tom." Neat differential. Tom was one of the men, she was only a secretary. She rose. "Of course," she said sweetly. "Poor old Tom. Can't make the ten steps to the coffeepot." She smiled at Tom.

Tom lifted his brows superciliously. "Women are kept home barefoot and pregnant, or, they go to work and make the coffee."

"I'll get the coffee." She gave Tom a diminishing glance and, predictably, Tom laughed. Mr. Blake did not.

Ah, she noticed with interest, so it was now "Mr. Blake" even in her mind. This job would never make it. And it was too bad, because she had been so comfortable here. He could be annoying her deliberately in order to make her quit. If she quit there'd be no suits or complaints filed. Perhaps he was bringing in his own secretary? Maybe his...mistress? "Sleep with me, babe, and I'll let you keep your job." That's what men did during the Great Depression in the 1930s. Her grandmother had told her about it. Mr. Blake would never say "babe." He'd say, "Well, Miss Moore, are you going to sleep with me, or lose your job?"

He could quite well be that businesslike about such an arrangement. Cold and self-serving. She looked down at the filling cup of coffee. Self-serving? Not if it was coffee. He was being extremely assertive right off the bat. While men are assertive, she thought, women are labeled as bitchy.

She smiled as she carried in the fresh coffee. "Too much coffee makes one irritable," she said so sweetly that Tom laughed. Again, Mr. Blake didn't. For a man of 33 or 34 he acted very straightforward.

She didn't replenish her own cup but sat down and was excessively alert, cheerful and helpful. Knowing the real Sarah, Tom had to cough several times to cloak a laugh. Mr. Blake appeared to expect just such behavior. He would.

Soon Mr. Blake and Tom were in shirtsleeves and had loosened their ties. They moved around now and then from the desk to the blueprints and schedules on the side table. Sarah watched them. Him. She wondered what it would be like to sleep with Mr. Blake. Well, having to call him Mr. Blake in bed would tend to be a remarkable formality in such an intimate encounter! She smiled, and then she had to cough.

Both men glanced at her and she returned a very innocent look. They went on with their discussion. That left her free to go back to her mental entertainment. She concocted a scene in which she stripped Mr. Blake's clothes from his body in order to get on with a seduction. He was stiff. Yes. But formal. She couldn't seem to get him into bed.

He rose then from his chair behind his desk, absorbed in his conversation, and shoved his hands into his pockets as he moved tired shoulders. Her eyes ran down his body. He was very nicely built. His shoulders were marvelous. His hands big. His stomach flat. He was very masculine. His thighs were like an athlete's. He was a powerful man. Uh-hmm. He'd probably be damned good—

"Miss Moore, can you do it?"

"I think I really could."

He looked a little blank. "Yes?"

"What?" she asked cautiously.

"Can you give Tom a list of the people who've applied as machinists in the past year?" He was looking at her oddly.

"Yes, sir." And she blushed. Redheads do blush. But she did it beautifully. Her skin was alabaster and the blush simply tinted her face with a rosy glow. She looked devastating.

Steven blinked and took a deep breath. Tom lay back in his chair and smiled at her. "Penny for your thoughts, Sarah."

She gave him a killing look.

"The list, Miss Moore."

"Can I send it down about—" she checked her watch "—four-thirty?"

"Fine. Good talk, Steven. Thanks."

"We'll get on this. And Tom, the reports on you are excellent. You'll be a good part of the team. You'll like the men you'll deal with. They're all exceptionally competent. This company is going to boom."

"Great!" Tom rose. "What will it be called?"

"It's still not settled. We'll continue to use the name Michaels until that's decided. Any problems, let me know."

"Thanks. Hustle up, Sarah, and you can go out the door ahead of me like a real woman."

"How special."

She had left her pad on Steven's desk. That and the tantalizing scrap sheet. He glanced out the door and she was out of sight over by the file cabinets. He went around the desk, opened the folder and pulled out the scrap paper. It was in shorthand. He'd learned shorthand in college in anticipation of law school. Not everyone could read another's symbols. Shorthand is like any handwriting, but Sarah's was clear and concise. It had read: Possible. Under that was *his* name, then various female names. Some had been marked through. Her name wasn't there. But then his name had been crossed off, and a large X had been put through the whole of it. Possible... For what?

Two

———

Friday wasn't any better for Sarah. She had to contend with the interim VP who was not old, but who was demanding, dictatorial, and wanted everything done five minutes ago. She worked like a dog. No, she worked like an exceptionally efficient woman. He took charge. Men take charge. Women take over.

The more organized and team-oriented of the personnel people had found a true leader in Steven Blake. They were exuberant. It was a pleasure to anticipate working with purpose and getting things done. Unfortunately there was the usual bitterly complaining and sniping deadwood whose routines were being rattled and whose jobs could well be in jeopardy. That part was unpleasant.

But the teeth-clenching part for Sarah was that Steven Blake deliberately pushed her to the limit. And she stretched to meet it. She faced him that night at five-after-five with everything he'd demanded done. Did he say thank you? No. He said, "See if you can come in a half-hour early on Monday. We'll need the time."

She refrained from replying. She said, "Good night."

He muttered something, not looking up. But when she turned and strode from the room, he watched her all the way out of sight.

He'd worked her hell-bent that whole day and she'd never faltered nor complained. She was a jewel. She was all her reports had said she was. No wonder old Taylor had lasted as long as he had. She was priceless.

She was also trouble. My God, what a woman! And redheaded. How was he ever going to solve this? The way she looked, he'd be up to his chin in her love affairs, quarrels, making up, and still have to cope with his own reaction to her. He'd have to get rid of her.

Sarah was in complete agreement without ever knowing what Mr. Blake actually had in mind. She drove to a local bar to meet the usual bunch of unmarrieds and newly marrieds who gathered there every Friday to celebrate the end of the week. Tonight she too would have cause to celebrate a week's ending! And that was after just a day and a half of "Old" Steven Blake.

"How is he?" She was asked that about a dozen times in the next hour or so.

Along with her knowledge of the department, her new boss came automatically into possession of her loyalty. Never would anyone hear one word of complaint from her about Steven Blake. So she replied, "I believe he will be very competent. He appears to be well-informed about this part of the company, and he already knows almost as much as I do about the key people. He's really boned up.''

"He's gorgeous!'' Joan told the rest. "Luke's lucky he has me tied down.''

One of the single males said, "Luke is lucky...period.''

There was a murmur of male agreement, and Sarah felt something that, in any other person, she would have thought might be jealousy. How could she be jealous of Joan? Could she be guilty of such an embarrassing emotion? She wasn't so trite as to envy her friends just because they loved each other so nicely? Yes.

The reactions to the week's turmoil at Michaels Inc. could be quickly slotted as the achievers vs. the deadwood. It was an interesting thing to watch and to hear. The malice. The whining. The excitement. The enthusiasm!

It made Sarah wonder which group she belonged to. She was in the middle. Neither excited nor malicious. Well, not verbally so. Her feelings of malice for Mr. Blake weren't of a business origin; they were strictly personal.

As she nibbled the baked and salted potato skins, the cheese cubes, and pretzels, she drank a diet drink for it was her night to drive and deliver people to their houses. That was a pain. No one wanted to go home. So she was stuck there until late.

She told Joan, "You stay in the car until I've delivered the men."

"No spirit of adventure?"

"None."

"Okay. Luke has night duty right now. Want to stay over?"

"I have to feed Mrs. Thompson's cat."

"It'll be asleep."

"And tomorrow I take the scouts out to Eagle Creek. Want to go?"

"I'd be delighted!"

"Would you now! Great! Can you get hold of Luke? Or leave a message so he'll know where you are? We can stop off at your place and get your things and you can sleep at my place."

"I'll go call."

So it was arranged. She and Joan arrived at Sarah's apartment about midnight, having turned down invitations of various sorts.

After they'd showered and were in pajamas they had two phone calls. The first was from Luke, "Just checking up." The other was from Steven Blake! At that time of night! Sarah couldn't believe her ears! He asked, "Would you be able to come in to the office tomorrow?"

With some deep pleasure Sarah responded, "Oh, I'm so sorry but I'm committed to my girl-scout troop for tomorrow."

To which he said, "Only girls? How sexist of you, Miss Moore."

She fumed for over an hour before she finally settled down to sleep—to dream fragmented dreams in which Mr. Blake did not play sympathetic roles.

There were fifteen thirteen-year-old girls in Sarah's troop. That's the age when girls *know* there is no way in this world they will ever look anything but sickeningly ugly. They were clumsy, because they had grown in spurts and now took up more space than they realized. They ran into and stumbled over things and were so precious to Sarah that she could have taken them all home with her. They returned her regard.

And there was Joan, who was a little subdued. In all the raucous maelstrom of arms
and legs and messy hair, Sarah noted that
Joan was quiet. After the volleyball game, as
they lay collapsed under a tree while the
shrieking girls ran off to see who were in the
canoes over on the Eagle Creek lake, Sarah
asked Joan, "You okay?"

"Yeah."

"What's the trouble?"

"Nothing." That was said very pensively
as Joan looked sadly off into the distance.

"Well, good," Sarah exclaimed heart-
lessly. "Glad everything's okay."

"Luke called last night."

"I know, I was there. That makes you
sad?" Sarah was astonished.

"He was checking up on me."

"He was seeing to it that two idiot women
had reached safe harbor."

"He doesn't trust me."

"Have you given him cause not to trust
you?"

"Not . . . exactly."

"Not exactly? How not exactly?"

"I've not been answering the phone the first time he calls at night."

"Why?"

"I get lonely."

"Where do you go?"

"Nowhere."

"You're playing games!" Sarah accused with a frown.

"All my young years are sliding by."

"Join the club."

"By the time Luke begins practice we won't be the 'young marrieds' anymore."

"You're feeling sorry for yourself."

"Perhaps." Joan heaved a large sigh.

"You've never struck me as being particularly idiotic."

Joan pulled up a long blade of grass and ran her fingers along it. "Steven Blake is a very impressive man."

"Watch out there, woman."

"Are you setting your stamp on him?" Joan's green eyes pierced Sarah.

"It would make no difference to you, stupid, if I did or didn't want him. You're already stamped! And don't you forget it."

"You're so tiresome, Sarah. Everything's cut and dried for you. No middle places."

"You pay attention—" But the hordes were back upon them and the conversation was discontinued.

Mrs. Thompson's cat always had a snort of rum in his evening tasty bits. He'd become a little wobbly and think he could sing—like a lot of other males who lapped up sauce. That evening, Sarah listened as he lay flopped on the side porch making a god-awful noise, and she was forced to inquire, "You're not trying for the Met. Say you're not." But he took it as praise and tried harder.

As she watered the pots and pots of various plants, she suggested other outlets, but he'd been neutered and wasn't interested. He had probably never recovered from being named Lily Anna as a kitten. There's no way to alter the name although he had been altered.

On Sunday, Sarah went home for the monthly gathering of the clan. It was always hectic. Auntie Tina was astonished every month that Sarah wasn't married *yet*! And that delighted her redheaded brothers. Her younger sister was black haired like her dad and she was so busy with her own life that she came only to eat and run, and left Sarah to help clean up. Sarah didn't mind; she enjoyed the time that gave her with her parents.

"What's it like after the takeover?" her dad inquired.

"Wild."

"Taylor's out? I always wondered how he held on. What an idiot."

"He never interfered," she told them.

"Why rock the boat? He was a real goof-off. I saw him swimming out at the club every afternoon, when he should have been at work. He was lucky to have you."

"I'm lucky he gave me so much responsibility. Mr. Blake is pushing me to the wall with his demands. I don't know if he's testing me or trying to get me to quit."

"Why would he do that?" Her father's face was quiet.

"I don't know. Maybe I'm just tired. I'm sure after we become used to one another it will all settle down."

"You take a little getting used to, princess. He probably took one look at you and thought he'd glimpsed heaven. Now he's panic-stricken thinking his time has come!"

"I love prejudice." She went and leaned against him. Then she sighed. "How about going with me to take the girls to Turkey Run next month on an overnight?"

"We'd love it," her mother replied to that.

"How'd I ever luck out on parents like you two?"

Instantly her father replied, "I walked into the library and there she was, stamping books...the sunlight on her red hair..."

"I know the whole story. But the thing that boggles me is, I was floating around up there, completely dumb, without one clue you two were going to turn out this great."

"Just blind luck."

She dragged home just after five and there, on the front stoop, with Lily Anna sitting on his lap, was Steven Blake. She was doubly amazed! First, that he was there, and then that Lily Anna trusted him! It had been a long time since Lily Anna had so innocently given trust. Trust led to disaster. The cat *never* sat on laps. That's how Sarah greeted the man, "Lily Anna *never* gets on anybody's lap!"

"This tom's name is Lily Anna? He's had more than his share of bad luck," Mr. Blake said gravely.

"Well, he does get rum in his tasty bits."

"Meager compensation." He changed the subject. "As I understand it, Phil Terry took a leave of absence?"

"Yes."

"Where can I find his file?"

She turned from unlocking her door and looked at him. "It must be in the office."

"I need it."

"Now?"

"Obviously."

So she relocked the door, put Lily Anna inside his apartment with his jot of rum, and slid into Mr. Blake's car to go out to the office.

Steve found it annoyed him that she had given no indication at all that he was an eligible male. Seeing him, she hadn't smoothed her hair, or straightened her jeans or re-tucked her shirt or anything. Nor had she asked if she could change her clothes. He was silent as he thought of that.

She too was silent. In romances, this was the setup for a seduction attempt that *almost* makes it. She closed her eyes to hide such idiotic thoughts. Mr. Blake would never do anything like that. It would be unprofessional. She coughed a little closed-mouth, throat-clearing cough.

"How were the records handled when the news of the takeover came along? Any moved?"

"No. At least, not to my knowledge. Those in your office are locked."

"Mr. Terry is a nephew of Mr. Taylor. Right?"

"Yes."

"How was his work record?"

She wasn't going to give an opinion on anything like that. She wasn't responsible for Phil or for his evaluation. "I believe that will be in his folder."

Steven Blake was again silent.

Sarah tried to decide if he was irritated because she had avoided a reply. Did he think she was so stupid that she'd offer an opinion? She wasn't qualified to judge any other employee. She had opinions, but they were personal observations, not based on actual work experience. There were those she'd never hire, given the choice. Phil Terry was one. He was pushy but that was only how he'd been to her, it had nothing to do with job performance. She'd heard that he was a whiz at accounting. But she would never in this world have willingly come out to the plant alone with Phil Terry on a Sunday night.

So why did she trust Steven Blake? Well, she obviously wasn't his type. When he looked at her his eyes were hostile. Her dad said Blake was probably susceptible to redheads and was resisting. Her dad was so prejudiced that it never occurred to him that people could be incompatible with someone he loved. Prejudice is blind.

Steven would have come around automatically and opened the car door for her, but she was already out. He walked beside her perfunctorily. They were together, so he didn't stride on ahead but walked beside her.

He commented, "You're really quite short."

Since she was wearing loafers she did have to look farther up to his face. She replied, "But I'm all muscle." Since she was looking at him she could have sworn she saw just the glint of answering humor, but it was gone before she could be sure.

If he had humor, they might be able to work together. Two days weren't enough time to decide to pitch such a cushy job. She'd give him a week or two before she abandoned him. He might just be a little nervous too, with a new job.... Him? Nervous? Ridiculous. He was a power. Nervous men don't become powers. He knew exactly where he was and where he was going. Nothing would deter him.

If he ever married it would be to the right woman who had the right connections and who would behave properly. She'd have genetically sound children who would be raised by English-trained nannies. He'd see the children each day for twenty minutes before dinner. Why did that depress her? She narrowed her eyes as they walked along the corridor inside the plant and she decided it made her sad—for the children.

He opened the door to their offices and took a quick look inside before he allowed her to go in before him. That was strange. Why had he checked? There was security at the plant. Had he expected someone to be in their offices? Suddenly she felt uneasy.

The place always looked oddly waiting. It was as if it were bursting with temporarily dormant energy. One switch and suddenly the lights and machines would waken and magically the people would be there to attend them. The machines controlled.

She blurted, "Machines baffle me. With my first car, I tried to put the oil into that little place where it's measured. It seemed a logical place to me." This was one of her tests. How men reacted to that gave her a gauge for measuring their attitude toward women. She admitted it was unfair. It tended to make men indulgent.

Mr. Blake gave her a glance and replied, "I probably would have, too, but my dad showed me how."

Quite honestly she then said, "I have trouble with machinery. The first time I turned on the new computer, a jet shrieked by over the plant, and at the same time there was a sonic boom. I was a total basket case. That was four years ago. It still takes courage every morning when I turn it on; I'm braced."

He pushed up his lower lip and considered her for a minute but he didn't laugh out loud. He was a first. Maybe he wasn't so dense about secretaries after all?

But then, on that Sunday, he put her to work and she worked flat out until ten that night, and all she had was a glass or two of water. He worked right alongside, and they hardly said a word. They never found Phil Terry's folder.

At ten she looked at the clock and sagged. "I'm finished. I'm seeing double and my back's broken. I'll never walk again."

"You want to go home," he guessed with what might in any other man have been droll humor.

"I see a glimmer of intelligence in you." She gave him a scathing glance and his face looked harsh under the fluorescent lights. Hers probably looked ghastly.

"Let me call security so they don't panic when they check the offices, and I'll take you home."

"I could walk."

"No need. It's on my way."

"This is triple time."

"You're on salary not wages." His voice was cool. "Working odd extra hours is one of the perks."

He had the gall to say that to the top secretary of personnel? If she wasn't so tired she'd throw the folders at him. But then she'd have to pick them all up and resort them. She flopped in her chair and leaned her head back as she waited.

He could hardly tear his eyes away from her. He was at his desk, talking to security, and he could see through the door to where she waited at her own desk, lying back, her red hair tousled and untidy from their evening's work. Her long denim-covered legs were sprawled so gracefully, and her elbows rested on the chair arms. Her round breasts were enticingly molded against her blouse.

They exited the building, and he put her into his car. "Are you hungry?"

"No thanks."

And they didn't say another word. He walked her to her door and stood until she'd unlocked it. "You didn't need to wait."

"The parking-lot kid might have been here." He'd deliberately called Louis a kid.

"Good night."

He didn't reply. He only lifted one hand and went back to his car and drove away.

She took a good, deep, soaking bath and drank a glass of milk before she crawled into bed at eleven. She slept heavily and dreamed Mr. Blake made love to her—almost—there among the littered files on the floor of his office. In it she frowned and thought what a ghastly chore it would be to pick them all up and refile them. He reminded her that she was the one who had tempestuously flung them at him in a temper because she was kept so late. He'd laughed and said he didn't care anything at all about Phil Terry. The search for the folder had been a ruse to get her there alone! Tired women had strange dreams.

The next morning, feeling quite refreshed, Sarah put on a new navy-blue silk blouse with white polka dots, and a navy silk suit and her usual high heels. She put good-looking pearls in her ears, pulled her red hair back with a navy ribbon and admitted she looked okay. Just as she was going out the door the phone rang. It was Louis. "Have you missed me?"

"I've got to rush. Take care." And she hung up.

She arrived at her office at exactly seven-thirty as Mr. Blake had requested on Friday, and her computer was uncovered and turned on. She figured he'd used it for something. He was there at his desk. Their eyes met and they both nodded formally like jousting knights just before they clashed. Neither said anything.

She looked so gorgeous that he almost fell over backward, chair and all, although he didn't move. He took a deep breath, and settled down eventually. Then she came with the mail and he watched her walk toward him with that marvelous stride, but she was wearing a jacket, which blocked most of his view. She didn't mention the fact that she hadn't needed to turn on her computer.

The new teams from the parent company in Chicago were tactful and patient. That's what all the people exclaimed about at lunch in the cafeteria. Sarah couldn't believe her ears. "They said to go along as we have until they become acquainted with our methods. If any changes are made, they'll be done gradually."

"Who said that?"

"It came in that nice note from your boss. Didn't you type it?"

"No. One of the other typists must have. He said we'd all begin slowly?" Sarah was having trouble assimilating that part.

"Isn't that thoughtful? I was with old Mr. Able when Michaels took this plant over and there were file changes, and clearings, and late hours and tempers! It was terrible!

These new people are so patient and friendly, and that makes it very nice."

Someone else put in, "And they say if any jobs are eliminated, we'll all find places somewhere in the network. That's a relief. I was afraid, being the age I am, that I might be squeezed out like Mr. Taylor."

So, Sarah thought angrily, everyone is being treated kindly and given time and not pushed? What about her? How long did an "interim" vice-president stay around? He wasn't treating her very well. He appeared prejudiced against her. It couldn't be her job performance; the files were kept up-to-date, and her work never lagged.

Yet Mr. Blake had run her tail off in the two working days he'd been there. He'd called her after midnight on Friday to work on Saturday and was at her house on Sunday evening, holding Lily Anna, waiting to drag her back to the office. Like Simon Legree in *Uncle Tom's Cabin*. But it was Steven Blake who'd written that tactful, soothing letter! It must have been a proxy who wrote it. Why hadn't she gotten a copy? Steven Blake was a two-faced slave driver. All sweetness and light to everyone else and secretly cracking the whip over her.

And she saw herself with her yellow slicker on over her belly-dancer's costume, barefoot, with bells around her ankles, cringing as he cracked a whip over her head and demanded she remove the raincoat.

"Sarah."

"Hmm?" Sarah looked blankly across the table at Joan.

"Where have you been?"

"Well, you mean this weekend?"

"Just now. You were a hundred miles away."

And one of the older women giggled and said, "She's daydreaming about that new boss of hers. Isn't he a dreamboat?"

"A hunk," one of the younger women corrected.

Sarah blushed because she *had* been thinking of Steven Blake. "He looks like he'd take a woman only to fill his need and never quit looking around for danger..." Her tongue stopped. Her blush deepened because movement made her look up at Steven Blake going slowly past her table right at that very minute, as if conjured by some evil genie. He looked straight at her. Good God, had he heard that stupid conversation? Not if her guardian angel was on the job.

All the way back to her office she quarreled with her guardian. She pointed out all the times it hadn't been around and she'd had to muddle—alone—through endless disasters that had been no fault of hers. If there was any sort of grading system, the guardian had better start shaping up. Heads would roll. That led her to wonder how one beheaded an errant guardian.

So by the time she was back in her office she was so involved with mentally figuring a way to really threaten her guardian that she wasn't nearly as nervous about confronting a possibly eavesdropping boss as she would have been right after lunch. Imagination does help. True, it can give one the heebie-jeebies, like just reading the title *Don't Look in the Basement* just before having to go down into one to put the clothes into the dryer, but there are times when imagination does help. This time it had distracted her.

So when she finally had to go into Mr. Blake's office, she could look at him quite calmly, as if she hadn't actually been at that table with those loose-tongued and silly-thinking women who considered Steven Blake a dreamboat and a hunk. Appearances could be deceiving.

As she came into the room, one of Mr. Blake's cohorts from the parent company was there. He looked quickly at Sarah and automatically rose to his feet as he finished speaking, "...there's some problem?" Then he smiled at Sarah so warmly and with such friendliness that she returned his smile quite recklessly. She wasn't used to being smiled at in that room, and it had taken her by surprise. The man blushed, grabbed his tie and almost inaudibly Mr. Blake said, "Down, boy," while he gave Sarah a cold, quelling look.

Problem? Her? If he hadn't wanted her to come into the room, he could have closed his door. He never closed the door. She lay the papers on his desk and started to leave. Mr. Blake said, "Miss Moore, this is our head accountant, Ted Zink."

Ted gave her his polished "I'm devastating" smile and held out an eager hand. She gave Mr. Blake a still look and said a grave "How do you do?" to Ted as she took his proffered hand. Then she had to work to get him to release it. Some men are entertained by shaking a woman's hand vigorously in order to watch her breasts bounce. Mr. Zink simply didn't realize what he was doing. And all the time Mr. Blake watched her—not the wiggling accountant who was acting like a lonely dog who'd finally found a friend— but her.

He also watched as she turned and left the room, walking away from him. Then he said to Ted Zink, "Do you want a cold shower?"

"I'd heard about her and I swear to you I was prepared..."

"I noticed."

"Now Steve, reality is stunning. How do you manage? Or is she...?" His tongue stopped dead in his mouth and dried out as Steven's warning eyes nailed him. Ted said, "Uh, oh."

Quite formally Steven laid it down cold. "She is a good secretary. She's businesslike, efficient and a lady. You behave."

"Check."

So the word went out not to put the make on Sarah Moore. Look, but with respect, and don't be stupid enough to try to touch. Sarah was a lady and, anyway, Steven Blake was too big, hard and tough to risk it. All that, along with the fact that he was a power in the company.

Poor Steven Blake. He really thought he was only doing that to protect Sarah Moore from being annoyed. He just didn't realize what was happening to him.

Three

———

As soon as he could find another place for her, Steven Blake was going to get rid of Miss Moore. Any man knew that redheaded women were Trouble with a capital *T*. And one with alabaster skin, which Miss Moore probably had all over her body, was the worst kind.

Then there was the Blake susceptibility. His dad's doctor had employed a redheaded nurse. She'd take his dad's blood pressure and it would go sky-high! Then he'd have to sit around for an hour and a half until it calmed down enough for the *male* doctor to get a normal reading.

Steven recalled quite clearly the third year that happened. His dad was so late returning from his yearly physical that his mother had become uneasy. When his dad finally got home she asked, "Are you all right?"

His dad's eyes had smiled and he'd slowly shaken his head as he replied, "It was that redhead who took my blood pressure again. It took two hours to get it calmed down."

His parents had laughed together softly, for his mother knew that had happened each of the two years before. "Does she flirt or joke with you?"

"Not a bit! She's completely professional. She doesn't even smile! She's businesslike and brisk. She doesn't do one thing. She's just there, breathing, and she's a redhead."

Since his dad truly loved his mother and he was a faithful, non-flirting man, she wasn't jealous. The next year, when he came home promptly from his physical, she asked in some surprise, "You're cured of red-heads?"

"She's no longer there."

"How awful. Do you know why she left?" His dad shook his head. "I wonder if they told her why she couldn't work there anymore. If she affected you that way, she must have wreaked havoc with a good many men. I wonder what happened to her?"

The fate of the redheaded nurse remained a mystery, but having met Miss Moore, Steven Blake now suspected she'd been dragged off over some man's saddle and spent her days locked in a hidden tower. God made women like Miss Moore for one purpose and men knew instantly what that was. At least the Blake men did.

Miss Moore wore high heels as if she were born in them. She walked with a lovely stride. She didn't bend her knee and put her foot down flat or mince along, but she naturally walked heel and toe as if she'd never walked barefoot. He was becoming an expert on the manner in which Miss Moore walked.

He lived in a state of half arousal and was exasperated that she should affect him so. He hadn't had such a problem since he was seventeen. He took to wearing pleated trousers and when he stood up, he became used to sliding his hands into his pant pockets.

As with his dad's encounters with the redheaded nurse, Miss Moore gave him no encouragement. She was firm, professional, efficient, and quite aloof. She was driving him crazy. Finding another place for her was like trying to get rid of a hot potato. While figuratively tossing her from one burned hand to another, he sought any reasonable transfer for her in the extended company.

However, she appeared to affect every other man in the same way. He simply couldn't allow her to have to contend with an avaricious man. He didn't try to figure out why not. He only knew, as an officer from the parent company, that it was his responsibility to protect her.

He was smart enough not to dump her on a married man, or too young a man, but—as with the nurse—age didn't seem to matter. As he would introduce potential bosses to her, without doing anything, she set them absolutely nutty. No man could act normally. They all grabbed their ties in varying grips and smiled their "I'm devastating" smiles as they said variations of "Well, hel-*lo* there!" It was disgusting. Fortunately he was in control. He was the least boggled by her...magic? Is that what it was? Well, at least *he* could control his response.

It wouldn't be fair to fire her just because she made men act like fools. She *was* efficient. It would be a shame to discard her just because she couldn't help how men responded to her. But as a gentleman, he couldn't submit her to the harassment that would be hers in any other office. He would simply have to settle down and endure.

As he studied her it became apparent that she really didn't understand her impact on men—or women. New female employees treated her as if she were Typhoid Mary. It wasn't until they came to know her that they gradually realized that she didn't like idle flirtation, and she was a good woman. That had surprised him, too.

She allowed no liberties at all. She didn't dress as a flirt and her makeup was minimal. She was cheerful, humorous, and treated everyone quite naturally. It was none of it her doing. But men had hellish problems adjusting to her.

"How do you survive?" One or another of his old team would inquire after meeting Miss Moore. He still couldn't bring himself to call her by her first name; it was too intimate.

He would ask, "In the new office? It's like any other."

"No, with that secretary! My God, man, how can you think straight?"

And he would look through the doorway at that stunning woman and reply, "It's just a matter of concentration. She's quite efficient."

But to a good friend whom he could trust, he said, "Rigid discipline."

The reply from his trusted friend had been heartfelt sympathy but it came in rueful laughter.

With great curiosity, Steven watched the men who'd been around Sarah for the years she'd worked there. She was the one who set the pace. She treated them as if they were normal and they all reacted to her with reasonable, surface decorum. But the men's faces were very vulnerable when their eyes rested on her. If she was a contender for a throne, she would have had loyal, to-the-death followers. Steven sighed at that thought. He would probably lead them.

If he could just sleep with her once, he'd find she was actually just like any other woman and he'd be cured of her. He'd looked up her records to find she'd never married. He was surprised that anyone who looked as she did could still be single.

She was probably cold. That was why her skin was so white. It was so frozen from the inside by her iced core that the sun could never warm her enough to tan her hide.

Steven decided there was no way she could be a virgin. Not at her age. Some man, some time had to have been overwhelmed and seduced her. He hated that man. He glared at the wall behind his desk with narrowed eyes and thought of all the mayhem he would commit on anyone who had done that to

Sarah Moore. Moore. If there was any more of Sarah there would be chaos at Michaels Inc. It was just a good thing Steven Blake was in control.

"If you had a window in that wall," Miss Moore's lilting voice interrupted his disruptive thoughts, "you would be able to look out over the beautiful Indiana countryside and let your eyes rest as you work your brain."

She had walked into his office and he'd been so deep in thoughts of mayhem that he'd missed the opportunity to watch her come to him. He swung around as she lay papers on his desk. "Are you a native of Indianapolis?" Even to his own ears it sounded like a standard pick up line.

"I'm the only native in Indianapolis," she replied easily.

He smiled his "I'm devastating" smile and said, "I'm from Ohio."

"I don't believe I've ever known anyone from Ohio."

"We stay home because no one has found anyplace better than Ohio."

"But you live in Chicago."

He gave her another shot of his sexy grin and waited for it to whammy her. Of course she would be immune. She'd been on the receiving end of those smiles since she was two years old. He watched her as he gave her yet another. She didn't turn a hair. He'd had women groveling with a second one, panting and clawing with a third. This was going to take time.

He should start by making a friend of her. That would throw her off guard. Then he could move in. He went through the papers blindly as he thought about moving in on her. Then he went through them again.

"Aren't they all right?" She seemed a little surprised.

"I wasn't paying any attention. I've been trying to solve a problem and I was distracted. I'll go over these in just a minute or two."

"Fine." She turned and he got to watch her walk out of his office.

It was quickly apparent that if he intended to try for friendship, he was going to have to quit watching her. He tried it assiduously for the rest of the week but gave up on Friday because the weekend was coming up. He would have no excuse to see her again until Monday and he needed to look his fill so he could last out the weekend.

"What's the matter?" she asked finally. "Is my makeup off?"

"Do you wear makeup?" He could forbid it. Make her look plain until they were alone.

"A little blusher. My skin's so dead."

Dead? That living alabaster? She thought she looked dead? He *almost* touched her. "Don't you tan at all?"

"No. I burn."

So was he. Burning. What if he simply laid it on the line. He could say: Look, I need to go to bed with you to get you out of my system; otherwise I'm going to have to fire you or transfer you, and if I transfer you I will go crazy trying not to think how some other man is trying for you.

She'd probably heard that same line a million times. Certainly she'd been told that it was her fault a guy was out on his ear and that she ought to help him. Most likely that was what the guy in the parking lot was trying for the first day. "That guy in the parking lot ever give you any more trouble?"

"Louis? He's under the mistaken impression he's in love with me. He isn't. When some men first meet me they can be rather weird. My dad told me to ignore them, it's my hair. It was Dad's idea that I learn judo. But after men know me, they settle down and realize how ordinary I am. It's always a chore at first, waiting for them to get through the preliminaries. My mother is redheaded too, but I didn't get her temper. She can make a man back off right away. I haven't yet learned how to do that. It's a nuisance. Louis is one of the persistent ones. I don't understand what he sees in me." She sighed in annoyance. "He's impossible."

"What do you mean?"

"Impossible for me. I could run him too easily. And his mother would be a contender for his whole attention. You will recall that he came by for a confrontation in the *morning*. His mother checks on him after work. He isn't even a Possible for me."

That "possible" sounded a bell. "A . . .

Possible?'' She had put that above his name that first day, before she crossed him out.

She replied quite openly, ''That's the first step. Then they become Probables if things click.''

''For what?''

She looked at him as if he weren't too quick. ''Marriage.''

In some shocked awe he quoted, ''A man picks a woman like an apple picks a farmer?'' It was a little frightening. ''My father raised me on that saying. Are you telling me it's true?''

Her look was kind. Sympathetic. He realized he'd failed in some way. She explained gently, ''It depends on the man.'' And she walked out of his office away from him. Had she once considered him a Possible?

She heard nothing more about any ''problem'' so perhaps it wasn't her after all. Mr. Blake didn't seem any more hostile, and every now and again he appeared almost friendly. Well, tolerant. There was the chance they would eventually rub off the rough corners and manage. The thought of rubbing off rough corners with him caused her to sigh quite interestingly.

So they had managed something like a truce. He had accepted that he was responsible for her and she would remain as his secretary; she had apparently adjusted to him, although she continued to call him Mr. Blake. Therefore he had to keep calling her Miss Moore. He'd begun the formality to protect himself, and now she was using it to keep him at a distance.

After the second week, amid almost constant, urging phone calls and even drop-by visits of the Possible Club members, Sarah gave the first party. It was going to be a casual thing—cocktails and nibbles, just to give the locals a look at the new blood.

Joan asked her, "Are you going to invite Steven?"

"I don't think it would be fair to invite Mr. Blake. He isn't at all interested in women. Have you ever seen him stop and chat with any of the women? Not for a minute. He might have a lady in Chicago. I would hate to expose any woman to him and have her fall for him and him not respond."

"How civic-minded of you."
"Yes."

Sarah had always given good parties and her place would be nicely crowded, but this time it was packed. She'd issued a singles invitation, and of course everyone showed up along with other Possibles. Most of the men were waiting for some of the regulars to get married and make room for new women in the club. But they were good company and were almost members because they would bring other men along. They brought some doozies. Men tend to be very careful whom they introduce to a bunch of eligible women; they're reluctant to bring in competition.

It was with some shock that during the party Sarah looked up and saw Mr. Blake sampling the goodies on the table. The place was jammed. There wasn't as much cigarette smoke as five years ago, but it was thick enough. Sarah squinted, not believing her eyes, but it *was* Steven Blake and he was there in her house! And he was shoulder deep in women who were acting like fools! How embarrassing.

Joan came along then and Sarah said in a scandalized voice, "That's Steven Blake over there!"

Joan smiled. "Yes."

"How did he get here? I was very careful he didn't know anything about it."

"I asked him. But . . ."

"You?"

"But he already knew about it. There could well be other uninvited men here, and even some marrieds. Parties are scarce these days. No one wants to go to the trouble and you do them so brilliantly."

So did Steven Blake. He took a long turn as bartender. And Sarah suspected some of the wine had been brought by him and perhaps Ted Zink. The two men mixed easily. They knew their way around women. It made Sarah feel very strange. Almost like when Joan said how magical it was being married to Luke. Almost as if she were . . . jealous of the women who talked so easily to Mr. Blake, and she watched as he smiled at them. He had never smiled at her that way.

Speaking of Joan's magical marriage, what was she doing chatting flirtaciously with Ted Zink? Sarah went over and stood by them for a while and was ignored. So she discreetly pinched Joan.

Joan said, "Ouch! Why did you do that?"

Through her teeth, Sarah snapped, "I could use some help in the kitchen."

Ted immediately offered, "I'll help too," and did. So they moved around as Sarah had intended Joan to do.

At two in the morning, there were still stragglers left at her before-dinner-cocktail party. About eleven some of the men had ordered pizza, and the party had gone on. Sarah was ready to ignore the hangers-on, crawl into bed and go to sleep; but Mr. Blake was still there.

Several times Sarah had seen Mr. Blake look at her, and now she saw he was moving deliberately toward her. He'd not greeted his hostess. Since she had no idea what to say to him, she'd been avoiding him.

As an indication that the party was over, she began to empty ashtrays into a metal can, and carry dishes to the kitchen. Mr. Blake helped, and it was inevitable that they met in the kitchen doorway. She looked up. He was in shirt-sleeves with his tie undone. He looked gorgeous. She wanted to walk into his arms and lay her head on his chest.

He was looking at her with that inscrutable stare and said solemnly, "You give great parties."

And she replied the stock answer, "Parties are the people you invite."

"You neglected to invite me and I'm single," he said seriously.

"I'm sorry." She hedged.

"An oversight?"

She shook her head minimally as she pushed back her unruly hair. That way she didn't have to out and out lie.

He told her, "I'm glad I got to come. You have a nice apartment. An interesting collection of furniture."

"It's called Vintage Relative Attic."

"I have some of that."

Her knees were weakened by the later hour or something, and she leaned against the doorjamb. He leaned against the other side.

She thought, standing there, they could very well appear to be old friends. Appearances are deceiving.

He moved his hand and tucked back some of her errant strands of hair. It was the most erotic thing that had ever been done to her, and she almost swooned under its electric impact! His hand trembled. Was it the late hour or could he be a little drunk, she wondered, although she knew he hadn't had that much.

He became even more serious. Her hair was exactly the silken threads he'd imagined them to be and they appeared to cling to his hand. Against his will his hand moved to her bare shoulder. Her alabaster skin was warm to touch. He had to straighten and put his hands in his trouser pockets and take a deep breath.

Since Mr. Blake was looking around, Sarah did too, and she saw small groups or couples talking low and laughing softly. The stereo was playing moody music, low and insidious. She thought that with a few palms set around, it might look like a brothel meeting-room. It was that kind of pairing up. A little more formal than that and no money involved, just marriage.

The women in the group weren't dumb. There had been a couple of bed hoppers, but they'd been weeded out. It wasn't the purpose of the club simply to find men; they all wanted husbands. All but Sarah. She had given up.

Mr. Blake said, "I've not been to such a nice party in a long time."

"Too busy?"

"No, I've had to attend mostly civic or corporate affairs. This is so casual, there's no one I have to talk to or need to entertain. And it's in a home. Most business entertainments are held somewhere else. I've missed being in a home. This is very special."

That made her feel like a rat for trying to exclude him. "I'm glad you could come."

The phone rang and one of the men answered. He said, "Hold on. Sarah? Someone for you."

She took the phone and said, "Hello?"

"Sarah, is Joan there? Do you know where she could be?"

"Luke! She probably couldn't get hold of you. She's here. Just a minute." She turned and called, "Joan, it's...your husband." Sarah felt a lick of unease. Joan was curled up on a couch, talking to Ted Zink. She got up lazily, smiling down at Ted in something other than a casual way, and she moved to the phone.

Sarah didn't go back to Mr. Blake. She began to pick up plates and gather paper napkins into a trash bag. She also listened to Joan talking to Luke. Joan's tone was defensive. A little arrogant. Challenging? Was it only a couple of weeks ago Joan had thought being married to Luke was a marvel? What on earth was happening to them?

Mr. Blake was at her elbow. "What's troubling you? Was the call something to upset you? I can help."

She looked at him and knew it was so. He would fix anything. She said, "No. It's Joan's husband. He's an intern. Working nights."

"I'll warn Ted off."

"Joan and Luke are perfect together. But medical training takes so long. So much of their time is spent apart. He has such strange hours. And he's always tired. Not long ago she said their marriage was a marvel.''

"I'll handle it."

"How?" She looked up at him. She'd taken off her shoes and she was short for his height. She felt overwhelmed by him. Subdued by him. Dominated.

He smiled just a little, and it was the first really good smile only for her. He'd been giving all those other women that kind of smile all evening, now at last she had one.

She looked so vulnerable that he wanted to kiss her. It must have been from the late hour. Her makeup was gone, her hair was a delicious tangle, and faint blue circles were under her eyes. Her mouth... He took another deep breath and looked around. "Let's load the dishwasher."

Joan came into the kitchen. "Luke is home. He hadn't told me he had tonight off." She looked at her hands. She was lying. "So I guess I'd better get back. Ted can take me."

But Mr. Blake said nicely, "It's right on my way. I will." Then he said to Sarah, "I've had one of the nicest evenings in I can't remember how long. Thank you." He had ignored several attempts by Joan to decline his invitation, and he took her off.

The rest left after helping with the tag ends of clearing things up. And they all decided they'd meet the next Saturday for a picnic. They had decided on next week because Mattie remembered Sarah had the girl scouts the next day and wouldn't be able to go. Everyone agreed it would be rude not to include the evening's hostess.

After they were gone, Sarah found Mr. Blake had forgotten his suit jacket. She put her hand on it and smoothed it. Then she picked it up and put it on. It was much too large. She hugged herself, then she took it off and buried her nose in it. She inhaled his fragrance, breathing deeply of him with her eyes closed and a small smile on her lips. Steven.

She was almost past being tired. She turned out all the lights, and went for a deep soak in the tub, before bed. She slept but didn't even dream. She was safe and secure, covered with his suit jacket.

He got back as soon as he could, but everyone had gone. He sat there in his car and yearned to her in that dark house, in her bed, alone. She was alone? Had he noticed anyone waiting specifically for her? Not that his ferreting mind could recall. So she must be alone in there, naked, on her bed, her red hair fanned out on her pillow. Waiting for him? He wished!

He'd purposely left his jacket as an excuse to return. He wished his damned jacket was in the car and he was there on the chair in the living room in the jacket's place. If he was there, it would be no trick at all to walk down the hall and into her room....

They were like strange cats on Monday. They eyed and paced and checked. He was still Mr. Blake and she was still Miss Moore. As she noted her uncovered and switched-on computer, he told her that he had enjoyed the evening at her house on Friday.

She replied, "I almost couldn't get up on Saturday. I had to take my scout troop to the Children's Museum. You left your jacket." She'd pressed it and carried it on a hanger.

It looked quite different than it had Saturday morning—all rumpled from sleeping with her.

"So that's where it was." He'd tried all weekend to call her and had never been able to get her. She was being quite distant. This was really going to take a while.

Four

How did a man court a woman like Sarah Moore? Steven had never had to try to attract a woman, they'd always been underfoot and willing. Now, how could he court her and do it at the office. His own secretary?

Any problem is solvable. To find a solution one begins by dissecting the dilemma into understandable parts. Sarah's parts were certainly understandable, but her mind, manners and mystique baffled him. What would it take to attract her attention?

He'd thought that she'd at least be pleased and smile when he had security turn on her computer every morning before she arrived. She hadn't even noticed.

All the time-tested ploys were out with an office courtship. He could hardly bring her flowers, or candy or wine. He had to get her away from the office in order to work that way.

He spent that Monday night sitting in front of the VCR, his eyes busy with the re-run of last year's play-off before the Super-bowl as his brain plotted. It should be as simple as any other relationship. If he ig-nored his sexual desire for her perhaps he could see that she was simply another gor-geous woman. If he could just think of her as an ordinary human being his confusion might subside. It shouldn't be *that* hard. If he could settle down and consider her as a personnel problem, he could quit being so silly and think of her rationally.

He paced about his living room and put his hands through his hair. She was an employee and he was her boss and he needed to become more at ease with her. If it were a male with whom he wanted to be more comfortable he would talk to him about things that interested him. He'd ask the employee's advice on something the man knew about and give the employee an opportunity to shine. That's what he'd do.

So the next morning he said, "I need some advice. I wonder if you'd be kind enough to help me decide on my curtains... drapes?" He smiled helplessly and shrugged, nicely divorcing himself from all knowledge.

She immediately said, "You need Sharon Lexington. She's just started her own shop, and she really knows what she's doing. Wait a minute, I have her card." While he stood with his mouth opening and closing with efforts at protest, she went back to her desk, searched through her case, triumphantly extracted a card and returned to hand it to him. "Give me credit when you talk to her. You're the first referral I've found."

He inquired rather stiffly, "Do you get a kickback?"

Unoffended she replied, "Oh, no. Only she'll be pleased."

So he was back to plotting. He became somber and a little testy. How could he ask her advice again? She'd be suspicious that he was trying to lay a trap for her. It was true he was, but surely he could be subtle enough that she needn't *know* it? Then it would have to be something besides advice. She probably had a stack of business cards with everything covered. He tried to ferret out her interests.

However, she was a stickler for office conduct, and replied to his probing with polite yeses or nos. She then went back to the problems or duties at hand. She was excessively efficient—just when he needed a watercooler relationship to ease into things.

Ted Zink came in on Tuesday and said, with an expressive widening of his eyes, "Do you have time for a word?"

Steven said, "Shoot."

Ted looked significantly at Sarah sitting on the other side of Steven's desk and raised his eyebrows in inquiry. Sarah didn't laugh out loud but she had to bite her lip.

"The premise?" Steven asked in a cryptic way.

"I haven't anything solid," Ted replied. "But it's just possible." He made the oblique statement a decidedly telling one.

Steven leaned back in his chair and put a hand to slowly rake his fingers through his hair. "Keep on it."

Sarah got up, tidied her folder and walked slowly from the room, giving Mr. Blake time to tell her she could stay, but he didn't. She was curious. When the problem was first mentioned she had thought that it was about her, but there wasn't anything in her background that would cause those two men to have to "work on it." So she wondered what it was and who was involved. It had to concern some kind of trickery.

With her logical mind, she considered the problem. Mr. Blake had dragged her out there that Sunday to search for Phil Terry's file. Phil was an accountant and perhaps he'd fixed the books. Simple. Wild. She let the idea go. The takeover audit would have found any discrepancy. The mark of Sarah's honor was that while she surmised, and was amused by her imagination, she didn't gossip about her speculations.

Of course Steven blew the golden opportunity of including her in the unraveling of that tangle. He didn't ask her very knowledgeable advice, thereby becoming closer to her, as he longed to be. His failure to recognize the opportunity was due to his basic male-oriented view that men rule—that men are on top of a situation; women merely agitate.

That day, however, in the hall, Sarah ran into security during her coffee break. No one would ever mistake Mr. Effingham as a part of the brave first line. He was shorter than she and had a round waist that, when he saw her, he sucked in with considerable effort. He grinned, showing missing teeth.

She smiled. "How are you, Mr. Effingham?"

He wiped his forehead with a blue bandana before he replied in a chiding way, "Yer shoulda tole me yer dint like turnin' on that there machine. I'da done it fer yer all along."

Then she knew. "So you're the one who's been doing that for me. Thank you."

"Glad to. Enny time. Jest tell me. Whatever."

"You're very kind."

"Wimmen need to tell us men what they needs. It's good wimmen work," he said earnestly. "And they do a good job," he assured her, "but they's jest things men can do—and are *glad* to do for wimmen." Then he smiled beyond her and said, "Hi there, Steve. I jest tole her she shoulda tole us before 'bout thet machine."

Steven limited himself to a Thank-you.

"Enny time." Mr. Effingham gave a slick wave and went off down the hall, a little breathless until he could turn a corner and let his stomach relax back into place.

Sarah turned to her boss. "How kind of you to have that done for me."

"I would solve all your problems." He smiled at her the same very vulnerable smile of all her entourage.

But she was so used to seeing the same smile on most men's faces, that she didn't realize what it meant this time. He wasn't a vulnerable man to other women, only to her.

He invited, "Coffee?"

"Now you know perfectly well we can't go get coffee together. Gossip would flood the building and we'd be swept out on a wave of speculation that would burst out the side of the building. Of course, then we'd have windows."

"It's energy efficient." He used that excuse again. Men are practical; women tend to be frivolous...like the way they're always wanting to see outside.

"It's been proven that the most polluted places are tightly insulated homes. The air is stagnant and there's no escape for the sprays, cooking fumes and exhaled breaths."

He laughed indulgently.

"It's true."

"Let's go back to our office for coffee break."

"I'm meeting Joan in the cafeteria. Is there something you need to discuss?"

"Just to visit. We never have." He was casual.

"I need to see Joan. She's avoiding me. I need to read her the riot act. She's about to louse up her life."

He nodded, pushing up his lower lip as he stood there with his hands in his trouser pockets. He narrowed his eyes against the urge to scoop her up, carry her off to his car and drive somewhere out into the Indiana countryside and hold her there until she gave up.

She smiled nicely, unaware of his thoughts. "Thanks for having the computer turned on in the morning. That was such a thoughtful thing to do."

"He forgot yesterday so I did it." Good God, he thought, why did he have to tell her that? He felt like a kid wanting his share of the spotlight.

She gave him her real smile and he froze there, coping with its impact for a long time after she'd walked away from him.

After a meeting on Thursday, Steven returned to his office to find the plant's head electrical engineer with Sarah. Unheard and unobserved by Sarah, Steven stood in the doorway and listened as Sarah was explaining, "It's about here. I can feel it right now! You're *sure* there aren't any wires under the floor?"

The engineer smiled as men always did to her and replied, "They're all in the ceiling."

"I definitely feel it here in this room. Now. Don't you feel it?" She was businesslike and firm. "If there's a short and the building catches fire and burns to the ground, I want it in the records—fireproof ones—that I called this to your attention."

"Honey, there's no possible reason for you to feel any shock. The carpet's especially shockproof and with good cause. Hullo, Steve. Your secretary finds your office 'shocking.' What have you been doing to her?"

Sarah had turned to acknowledge her boss's presence, but indignantly turned back as the engineer went on talking. She saw the slow, lazy, humor-sharing man-smile he gave to Steve. Suddenly she realized the innuendo and jerked her head around to confront Steven's response to such a blatant accusation.

Steve's face didn't change from one of interest. Blandly, but with an underlying hardness, he replied in a dangerously mild voice, "Could there be a metal joining that's picking up some dissipated power? It might not be harmful, or produce a spark, but could it possibly affect someone walking over it?" He relaxed against the doorjamb but his words and attitude were a tough challenge.

The electrician soberly replied, "There's always that possibility. Miss Moore, I didn't mean to disparage your inquiry. I'd prefer to investigate a hundred unnecessary times than to ignore one. And I'll check this out. I would have anyway, but I really only meant to reassure you. I'm sorry if I appeared to take it lightly."

"No problem," Sarah assured him and serenely went back to her desk.

Steve asked the engineer, "If you have to take up the carpet, wait for the weekend, will you?"

"We'll use a metal detector right after lunch."

"I won't be out of the office until about two. How about after that?"

"Fine."

The engineer left. Under ordinary circumstances he might have gossiped about Sarah's plight, but not now. Not with Steven's serious protection of her. Even then, he might have shared the fact with one or two that Sarah Moore *was* susceptible to a man, but he wouldn't. Not now. It wasn't just his respect for Steven Blake; deep inside he was a touch romantic.

Steven waited an impatient five minutes before he said he had an errand and would be back eventually. Hurriedly he took off. He went out of the building into the early May day, and he was so exuberant that he almost could have flown! Did she *really* feel something like electrical shocks when she was around him? He was going to *get* her!

He drove with studied care to a hardware store and searched for the exact wire he would need. He had to haggle with the salesman because they didn't want to sell him just ten feet of it so he ended up buying the whole roll. He clipped off the ten-foot piece he wanted and left the rest. "If some guy comes in and wants only a part of a roll, you're on your honor to charge only for your time. Right?" The clerk laughed in response.

They didn't have a plain paper bag and he couldn't walk into the plant with a sack from a hardware store—or simply a ten-foot coil of wire—so he had to go around and try to find something in which to conceal it. He decided on a candy box. And this time he smiled.

At the office he removed the wire, ate a piece of the candy, offered one to Sarah, and passed the candy around the rest of the office.

So that afternoon the engineer and a helper did find a loose piece of wire imbedded in the carpeting and one end was near to an electrical circuit. He knew damned well it wouldn't cause a shock, but he was smart enough to express great satisfaction that the problem had been solved.

And Sarah was vindicated. Steven thought it was too bad he couldn't tell her what he'd done for her. If he did, he would be admitting he now knew she was affected by him. He would be confronting her with the fact that she was attracted to him.... It wasn't some forgotten wire that caused her to feel vibrations and excitations when she came to him. Steven Blake knew he was making her respond that way. He smiled like a cat with a canary feather on his whiskers.

So now, how was he going to get her to realize that?

She already knew. She knew it the night she slept with his jacket. That was an unarguable clue. But she hadn't known how bad she had it until she had the electrical engineer there in the office. She wasn't dumb. Trying to explain the sensation, not feeling it, then being jolted by it when she found Steven behind her made her realize the sensation was sexual attraction.

He must never know. He'd be so embarrassed. Uncomfortable. He wasn't marriageable material, and she wasn't for any casual relationship, no matter how serious it was. She wasn't the type. She refuted her attraction for him. She would recover.

But she dreamed. That night she dreamed of him. All out, madly, sensually, wildly. She awakened in a sweat, on fire, in a wrecked bed. This was physically ruinous. She'd have to change jobs.

On Friday she went into his office, now knowing perfectly well what caused her legs to react, her thighs to tingle, her body to respond. Just the smell of him made her dizzy and scattered her brains. He must never suspect. Thank God the electrician had found that wire! How careless the carpet people were to leave it there when they were laying the carpet. How lucky she was they had found something to explain away her complaint!

That night Steven went along with everyone else. He wasn't even subtle to the men with whom he communicated the fact that Sarah Moore was off-limits. He didn't tell her about his actions. However, he did ask her, "Do you really want a permanent relationship with a guy who cruises bars?"

"Would you have a relationship with a woman who cruised bars?"

"It's different with men," he responded, certain of this.

She looked at him with a rather irritated glare. He was so locked into male thinking. How could he be in personnel when he thought that way? Surprisingly enough, at work he really did a good job communicating, and he was impartial. But when it came right down to it, in his own life, mentally he was unalterably male. He'd think that men who acted less than honorably were virile, while the same kind of behavior in a woman should be considered nymphomania.

"There's the parking-lot kid over there, mooning over you from a distance." Steven was scornful.

"He's really a very nice man. It's just that, for me, he isn't a Possible. Excuse me, I have to call Mattie, to tell her he's here."

He muttered something about apples picking farmers and ordered another drink.

After making her call, who should she see walking in but Phil Terry! Now that was very interesting, for he'd been on his leave of absence for almost a month, and he hadn't been around at all since the takeover. It was as if he'd vanished. She'd surmised that all the talk of "problems" concerned Phil Terry. But would he be here if he'd bilked Michaels Inc.? Of course not. That just showed she had leaped to a wrong conclusion. Repulsive as he was, Phil Terry wasn't the "problem" Steve and Ted had mentioned.

Phil saw Sarah immediately. Who wouldn't, with that flaming-red hair? He knew she would be out with the gang on Friday and he was there deliberately to see her and to take care of unfinished business.

As she had once before, however, she made a beeline for the biggest and most formidable man in the room. "Phil Terry's here. Don't leave me," she said, squeezing in by Steven at the bar.

No name could have caught his attention quite like that one, but he was riveted by the fact that, again, she had sought his protection. The first time might have been happenstance, but this time she'd chosen him above all the men she knew. The idea was as heady to him as breathing pure oxygen. He smiled down at her as a cat would at a tasty mouse.

His expression made her blink. He'd never looked at her quite that way, and she had a fleeting thought of a frying pan and a fire, but scoffed at such an idea. She peeked up at him for a quick check, but his expression was bland. Perhaps she'd been mistaken.

"There you are," Phil said. "Hello, Sarah." And he smiled the woman-tested Terry smile.

From her shelter by Steven, Sarah said, "Phil." But she didn't smile back and she didn't actually greet him. She only acknowledged he'd spoken. Any other man would have taken the hint and gone on.

Typically Phil didn't. He reached out to take her arm and pull her out of the mass by the bar, but his hand was intercepted skillfully by Steven, who bared his teeth in a travesty of a smile and said, "So you're Phil Terry. I've been hearing quite a lot about you. I'm Steven Blake."

The name was not unknown to Phil and it caused him to pause. He said, "Yes," in a noncommittal way. Then he said to Sarah,

"Let's get out of here." He hit her with another of his practiced smiles.

"Sorry—" she began.

"She's with me." Steven made it very clear.

"Aren't you with the takeover group?" Phil inquired.

"Correct." Steven smiled smugly as he made the term "takeover" rift with another meaning.

"He's my boss." Sarah gave the original meaning back to the words, for she hadn't caught the double meaning.

Phil frowned at Sarah. "You've moved to marketing?"

Steven replied for her, "I've moved to personnel."

That seemed to surprise Phil. "Why would you leave marketing? You're the fair-ha—" Then he stopped abruptly since he didn't want to puff up a rival.

"I didn't leave marketing. I've taken up personnel for a period of time."

"Dating the boss?" Phil's eyes dropped to her chest. "Isn't that against your rules?"

Steven slid an arm around Sarah as he pulled her close to him. He didn't feel the need to reply, but neither did she. She was coping with rioting nerve ends because her breast was flattened against Steven's chest and all sorts of quiverings were carrying on throughout her body in utterly amazing sweet and liquid waves of feeling. It took all of her attention. Her eyelids almost closed, her lips parted, and her heart carried on quite astonishingly. She was probably going to lose consciousness. How nice he was holding her so she wouldn't hit her head on the floor when she blacked out.

Phil kept trying. "Why don't we go on out for supper, and I'll take you home." His eyes promised lots of things.

"No thanks."

"Come out of the crowd and let me talk to you. I've some exciting news."

"I'd like to hear it too." Steven politely bent his head and gave him a sincere expression. "You are coming back to work, aren't you?"

"I doubt it. With Uncle John retired, I thought I might travel with him for a while.

He's a fine man and he's always been very nice to me. I think I owe it to him to be around in these years when he can travel and see the world.''

"So you plan to leave the country?'' Steven's voice was placid and courteous.

"Not for some time. I want to see Sarah, if you will release her. We're old friends—'' he gave her a pithy look ''—and no longer working colleagues.''

"Not tonight." Steven was quite sure.

Phil considered how far he could push, and finally he used a smoldering voice and said to Sarah, "I'll call you." He reached out to touch Sarah's cheek, but just then Steven apparently reached for his drink, and in doing so, he turned; Sarah was moved in front of him and Phil's finger was brushed off by Steven's shoulder.

Of course it was deliberate. Cleverly, quickly done. She could have cheered, and she felt so glad to be protected by Steven. If she'd not been, Phil would have managed to "accidentally" brush against her bottom and her breasts. He'd always done that before, and it had always made her simply furious. He was the kind of man who laughed and hugged a woman when he said vulgar things—as if that made it friendly and acceptable.

Phil moved away, stopping and speaking to all the people from Michaels Inc. whom he knew. Apparently he was familiar with the names of the others as he was introduced or introduced himself. That's when he met Ted Zink. Steven was watching, and his eyes met Ted's.

"Let's leave," Steven said to Sarah.

"I'll go to Joan's."

"He knows you're friends so he'll go there if you aren't home. Let's go to my place. You can tell me if you like your friend's taste in drapes. I think they're a little wild. They startle me when I walk into my apartment. If I were Lily Anna and had had my tot of rum, I'd probably think I was getting the DTs."

As he talked, he moved her along with him, his hand touching her waist to guide her. All the Michaels Inc. people noticed, but with Phil there, they suspected she had merely sought shelter with Blake.

Sarah noted Steven's bland smile, but his eyes were excited and dancing. There was the frying-pan/fire syndrome again. But if Steven Blake was the fire, she preferred his fire to Phil's frying pan. She preferred Steven, period, but she ought not go to his apartment.

Then Joan approached them. "Good. Get her out of here. In fact I'll go with you."

Sarah felt Steven's arm muscles clench. She almost laughed. That wicked man! Surely he hadn't plotted her seduction? She reached for Joan's hand and the three of them left and got into their various cars and the two women followed Steven to his apartment.

Steven was living in Michaels Inc.'s courtesy apartment, which had been furnished with all the imagination of whoever invented canned music. Nothing jarring. Sarah mentioned, "I can see how you might want to do some redecorating. However, I doubt Michaels Inc. would appreciate your interference with this marvelously neutral decor. Just think how they must have had to struggle to get it all so bland. Even the pictures! And the totally unobtrusive fake flowers! How amazing!''

He watched her patiently, but he was amused she didn't mention that he had pretended to have hired a decorator.

At ten o'clock, Joan called Luke, and he asked to talk to Sarah. Sulkily Joan handed over the phone.

"Is everything okay?" Luke asked. "Joan says Phil was downtown. Was he giving you trouble?"

"Everything's fine. My boss was there and he brought us to his place. Joan's acting as chaperon so Steven's reputation won't be shot."

Steven was pouring them some wine. Listening, he heard as she called him Steven. Spoken by her, his name sounded exciting. He'd always thought it dull. A name to fit perfectly into something like the courtesy apartment. But she said it and it took on bravery and character and...romance. It was as if he wore armor and were fighting to put her back on her throne. My God, he was going crazy.

He grinned at Sarah and reached for the phone. "Let me talk to Luke." Then into the phone he said, "Hello, Luke. I feel I know you by now. Everything is under control. I could use a shotgun rider. When can I count on you?"

"In one more week."

"Good. I'll try to hold out. Take care. Don't kill off anyone important."

Luke replied automatically, "All mine are important."

"Right. I'll follow Joan home when I take Sarah back. Let me give you my phone number."

"Good. It'll give me another place to call when I'm trying to trace Joan."

"Not here," Steven told him. "I'm for the other one. And we're combined on this problem."

"Then you know there is one." It wasn't a question.

"Actually there isn't. It's a smoke screen."

"We are talking about Joan?"

"Yes."

Luke sighed. "I hope to God you're right. She's driving me nuts."

"No need. Trust me. The girls are safe."

"Do you mean Joan is for me?"

"I'd bank on it."

"I may adopt you into my family."

"I'll drink to that when I see you. Take care."

"Let me say good-night to Joan. I think maybe she should stay with Sarah tonight."

"I suppose. I'd be willing."

Luke laughed. "I'm looking forward to meeting you."

Steven's laughter was soft. "Here's Joan." He turned to the brunette beauty. "Want to take it in the bedroom?"

She gave Steven a careful look. "All right." And she left the room, taking her time.

"What was that conversation all about?" Sarah asked curiously, after Steven had hung up the extension.

He grinned. "What did it sound like?"

"I have brothers so I know men talk around things. Were you giving him messages about us?"

"I told him not to worry so much about Joan."

Five

Joan finished what turned out to be a long telephone conversation with Luke and rejoined the couple in the living room before they left Steven's apartment. They got into their cars and followed Joan to her house and left her car. Then she rode with Steven, and a strangely hostile Sarah followed them to an all-night parking garage where her car was to be stored for the night.

"This is brilliant," Joan said, now settled in the back seat of Steven's car. Sarah was in the passenger bucket seat as they drove to the Broad Ripple section of Indianapolis.

Steven explained, "He'll be looking for Sarah's car."

"He'll assume I've spent the night with you." Sarah put that in.

"Or Joan," Steven added. "We all left together."

"He'll *know* I spent the night with you. It's the way he thinks."

"I don't mind."

"It makes me a little uneasy. I've been very careful. He's a complete insect."

"Don't worry, I can handle him. This way you should get a good night's sleep. He'll be looking for cars and there won't be any there."

"He'll be unpleasant when he sees me again."

"I'll be around."

It was interesting to Steven how competitive he felt. Actually, his intentions toward Sarah were exactly the same as Phil's, but his were of a higher level. How? Well, if he was honest he would admit he wanted Sarah exactly the same way Phil did. In his bed. So what was different?

The difference was he wanted her to like it. He wanted her pleasure to match his. He wanted her to crave him and relish him just as much as he did her. And while the act was the same, there was a wide chasm separating taking a woman and making love to her. He wanted her struggling for him, not fighting to get away. He wanted her in his arms, in soft surrender, quivering with desire, not shaking in revulsion. He wanted her. And no other man would have her.

He didn't park right in front of Sarah's house but stopped down the street. He said, "Want me to come in and look in your closets and under your bed?" His words had begun teasingly, but as he said them he got out of his car, helped the two women out, and locked the doors.

"There are two of us," Sarah protested.

Joan said, "Let him."

"Well . . ." Sarah was slow to agree. "Okay. But be careful how you open the hall closet."

"Running out of storage space?"

"If Mrs. Thompson stays in England, I'm going to take her apartment and use it all as storage."

Steven nodded. "Don't turn on any additional lights," he cautioned as he took her key and unlocked her door. Then quite naturally he took up the storage problem. "You may well have pack-rat genes. I have some on my mother's side. It's strong in one sister. Her husband doesn't even keep a toothbrush. He can move across country in the clothes he's standing in." They walked into the silent apartment, and Steven began his tour. The two women followed along, as he continued his dissertation: "We came to the conclusion that God matches up people of opposite tendencies like that so genetic strains don't get too intense. It's tough on the first couple but it does produce diluted peculiarities and more balanced personalities in the children."

"You must have fascinating discussions in your family," Sarah commented.

"Everybody talks at once. You have to be very perceptive to get it all. I'm a listener."

In the back of the old house, in what had been the morning room but was now Sarah's bedroom, one of the windows was not quite shut. He only noted it wasn't locked. But Sarah was startled for she thought the window had been completely closed.

"You need some stops on your windows." His voice was quite calm although his nerves twanged. "It's very easily done. In fact I believe I've a drill in my tool kit out in the car. I'll check it. Do you have any nails?"

"What kind of nails?" Joan asked.

"Big ones. Three inches?"

"I'll look in the kitchen drawer." Sarah went on out of the room.

Joan said easily, "Everyone in the world must have a junk drawer in the kitchen. Is that genetic too?"

"Probably one of those traits that sneaked by early."

"Have you ever used anything from a kitchen drawer?" Sarah asked from the other room.

Steven replied in an oddly pensive way, "I've moved too many times to accumulate anything."

They heard a yowl outside and Sarah abandoned her drawer search to let Lily Anna inside. He was in a cranky humor because he hadn't had his rum.

Joan was used to Lily Anna, but Steven was opposed to giving booze to a cat. "Any vet will tell you that's not good for him."

"Well, I refused to feed him garlic and ..."

"Garlic?" Steven just touched the word in disbelief. "To a cat?"

Joan explained, "Rum keeps them from getting worms."

Sarah elaborated, "Mrs. Thompson vividly recalls a joke about a temperance meeting held in a tent. The preacher had two glasses. One contained water and in the other was the demon rum. The preacher put a worm in the water and it wiggled around and enjoyed itself, but then he put the worm in the rum, and it died. The preacher shouted, 'See? Do you understand what that means?' And at the back of the tent some lush wobbled to his feet and declared, 'If you drink rum you won't have worms!' Which must have broken up that meet."

Steven laughed nicely, considering how many times he'd heard that classic, and he said, "So Lily Anna gets rum."

Joan said virtuously, "Only for medicinal purposes."

And Sarah added, "No self-respecting worm would go near a garlicky, rum-soaked cat."

Joan watched the cat lapping it up. "I have no objections to him getting soused, it's his singing that I can't stand."

"He's practicing for the Met." Sarah lifted her hands out and dropped them in a way to show that practice would not help.

Joan yawned realistically. "I'm going to bed and put my head under the pillow. Behave, you two." She leaned down. "You too, cat."

Lily Anna gave her a disgusted look.

With Joan off to the second, very small bedroom, the two were alone, if one ignored Lily Anna who was tuning up on the kitchen counter.

"He ought not be up there," Steven told Sarah quite sternly.

"I know, but I scrub it before I use it."

"The rum is beginning to hit. He's going to be really drunk pretty soon and he'll fall off."

"He's been drinking long enough to know the hazards. He will have to take care of himself. I refuse to pander to a drunk."

"Then don't give him any rum!"

She gave him a patient look. "I water it. His response is mostly reflex. But if he doesn't get any, he sinks his claws into my leg." She showed him healing scratches. He resisted kissing them well.

Since Steven needed something to do in order to hang around for a while, he went outside to his car and got his tool kit. He drilled a hole in the top right corner of the bottom window, then he drilled another hole, four inches up from the bottom of the right side in the frame of the upper window. The window could be raised so the holes matched, a loose nail put through the matched holes, and no one could open it farther or close the window until the nail was removed.

There weren't any nails. "We have to find something or keep the window locked." Steven was emphatic.

She searched the kitchen drawers. He thought a skewer might not be strong enough; it might be broken. So she found a cocktail fork and they used that. A sterling-silver window stop.

He felt very satisfied. It was as if he'd introduced a crocodile into her moat. They went into the living room and he slung his jacket over the same chair he'd left it on the night of her party. Her eyes clung to it and she longed to go over and bury her nose in it to inhale the fragrance of his body. His skin.

She had him right there. She paused, struck by the thought. If she was a bold and forward woman, she didn't need his jacket! She could go and sit beside him, move over to kiss his firm mouth, then lean her face down and breathe of him.

She put her hands in her hair and looked at the floor until the dizziness passed.

His deep voice was low and very masculine. "You're not afraid, are you?"

She looked at him blankly until her mind sorted out whether she was afraid of herself or of him. Then she remembered the threat of Phil. "I'm quite strong. All muscle, if you recall. And I know judo. I'm quite good."

"In a studio." He reminded her.

"I haven't been able to find anyone who wanted to attack. I am intimidating." She swaggered and something odd happened in his chest.

"I'd be willing to attack you," he offered in a foggy voice. "Strictly for research purposes, of course."

"Well, that blew it. You warned me!"

She sat in the chair opposite the couch where he was sitting. There was a small silence, broken only by the cat's practice session. And she looked at Steven. He was sitting not six feet from her. She could surprise him, tip him over and fling herself on top of him, imprisoning him.

He asked, "Would you have any milk?"

Since her thoughts were so chaotically erotic, she smiled brilliantly and replied like a perfect hostess, "In the kitchen." She was startled that he grinned so widely as she rose to go to the kitchen.

As she poured the glass full, her brains scrambled around looking for things to talk about to distract her wicked mind's imagination. He was going to be with her long enough to drink the milk and it wouldn't do to sit there in silence. What on earth could she talk about?

But when she carried the glass back to him, he asked, "What are the Possibles? I understand they're a matchmaker group. Tell me about it.''

''It came about by accident. Some of us were talking about men we knew that, while we didn't want them, they were good guys. Someone else might be delighted with them. So we started out, just five of us, and we gathered women and men along the way, and it's grown to just about convention proportions now at our annual Fall Singles Party. Even if we aren't actually trying to match people up, the parties are great bashes. Fun. You'll... No, I understand you're a confirmed bachelor?''

''Yes.'' He smiled nicely, waiting for the expected, standard protest.

''I'm so glad.'' He blinked, but she went busily on, ''Men who are marriage oriented very rarely offer up any attractive acquaintances to the group. We do understand; why introduce competition into the group? They want as much scope of choice as they can get. I suppose that's natural. But we do have more women than men. When Natalie Unger was married, I asked for her list of Possibles, and she still wouldn't give it up! Makes you rather wonder how firm the marriage is, if she's keeping a list of Possibles, doesn't it? But you could help, since you're not interested. You know. Your friends. You do have friends? Younger men?"

That offended him.

"And single? A depressing number of men are married. Although there are some of those who will fool around, that's not what we want in Possibles. Do you know any unmarried men?"

The "younger" still rankled so he said smoothly, "My nephew."

"What's he do?" She smiled, very interested.

"He's unemployed."

"Oh?" Her face became blank.

"He's six."

He was being cute. Primly she went on, "Yes. Anyone above twenty-five? Frankly, the field is a bit picked over so we're always looking for men. Some are willing to marry but they don't know how to go about meeting women. Or while they might not be suitable for one woman, they could be perfect for another. Like Louis. Remember him? In the parking lot. Yes, him. He's very sweet. You may not understand his conduct, but he really wants to marry. Beth wanted a shot at him, but that would never do. She's too structured in her thinking. He might adjust to it and even enjoy her, but it wouldn't be true love, and his mother would *never* come around. One never comes between a mother and her son, if the mother is possessive. Mattie will do very well.''

''Too... structured?''

''You know. She's the type who might be unnerved if you ever wanted to act like a chimp in the bedroom.''

His eyes cast down to hide his hilarity from her earnest gaze, he bit his lip quite hard so he could soberly inquire, ''A... chimp?''

''Like Greystoke,'' she explained quite readily. ''Lord Greystoke who was Tarzan, you know. I'm not sure Beth would understand...''

He had a hell of a time controlling himself but he would not laugh. She was so serious. He had to move or he'd burst with laughter. So he got up and served himself some wine because he couldn't trust speaking in order to ask permission for it. He drank a sip and was still bordering on hilarity as his mind saw himself swinging around the bedroom, with Sarah, naked, her body so beautifully fancy, waiting for him on the bed. The thought of Sarah sobered him. He turned. "May I pour you some of your wine?"

"No thanks. Well, just a little. It's almost eleven. Tomorrow's the picnic. Oh, I haven't boiled the eggs!"

He followed her into the kitchen and leaned in the doorway to watch her as she busied herself with that brief chore, and he smiled as she leaned over the drunken cat and pretended to harmonize with his yowls. The cat didn't think she was getting it right and got louder as his eyeballs bulged with his annoyance over her intrusion.

The humans went back to the living room and sipped their wine. Steven gave her the opening, "So you do pay attention to matching up people with the same likes and dislikes?"

"We're not matchmakers; we only get Possibles together. We're not even a dating service. We invite people to places so they can meet. After that it's up to them. But there can be glaring inconsistencies. If we know that, we try to avoid disasters. However, we do find people in very different fields who match up quite well. Take Rob and Hattie. He's an amateur marathon runner, and she's a concert pianist. His running and her practicing take time. Lots of time. But she practices while he trains. And she is exercise conscious while he likes her kind of music. It was ideal. Most of the matches are ordinary, with the usual horrendous adjustments."

"That almost sounds as if you're not entirely sold on marriage." It was interesting how such a confirmed bachelor waited for her reply.

"I gave up the idea." She sighed deeply and in watching her chest sigh, he lost his turn to speak. So she went on; "I've never been a career person. I'd been saving for down payments—on a house and a second car—collecting silver and crystal..." She moved a hand in circles to include all those preparations to share a life.

"You never found the right man?" He was awed. She had *wanted* to marry. She hadn't wanted to spend her life as a Lorelei, luring men to disaster with her alabaster skin and flaming hair.

"I'm twenty-nine!" She allowed him time to be amazed, but it was difficult as he'd looked up her records long ago when he'd had nothing to do for two seconds. She then added, "I've been using the silver now for two years, and I've had to actually replace one of the goblets." Then she shared new wisdom: "One finally gets past the age of orange-crate bookcases and picnic steel. It seemed a pity to allow all that stuff to lie around useless, wrapped up in blue paper, to be inherited by my nieces. So I dug it out and had the first party. I invited all my single friends. It was an omen. I'm unmarriageable." She could admit that to a confirmed bachelor.

"The parking-lot kid—" Steven had a tough time discounting any man's persistence.

"I've already told you we're totally unsuited. The day will come when he'll be glad he escaped. His mother would never have relinquished him to me and I'd want a husband to give me equal time with his mother. Not total time, just equal. As I said, Mattie will manage nicely."

"Mattie . . ." Steven was a little unsure.

"She's the one who has the next chance at Louis."

"Why were you and Louis unsuited?" It was the first time Steven hadn't called Louis "the kid."

Quite frankly she confessed, "I would rule him. It would take an unusual man to marry me."

"One who disagrees?"

"No, of course not. Who wants a contentious man? Or woman. I'd need an intelligent man who used his mind against my contrariness. For I *would* test him. He would have to be a man who couldn't be led against good sense, but wouldn't lose his sense of fun. If I said tomorrow the sun will rise in the west, Louis would believe it. The man I'd marry would turn the house around so I could pretend to be right."

"So you've sorted us through and find us lacking." The confirmed bachelor included himself as an us?

"And not even faithful!" She gave him a glinting grin. "Men are so fickle. One told me he'd never love another woman, and now he's married and they have *two* kids!'' She laughed.

He smiled in the dim light reflected from the night-light in the kitchen. He was lying back on the sofa like a sultan being amused by a candidate for his attention. ''So what would attract you now? Since there are no perfect men?''

''Oh, there are perfect men. It's just that none has come my way. And the several who might have proven perfect, I've never tried for because they were already married.''

''Would it take money?''

''That's crass.''

''Someone not around much?''

She took it up, laughing deliciously, ''Just long enough to give me some babies. I would like children.''

''You'd just want him around occasionally to impregnate you.'' His breath came a little quicker.

She agreed, with droll humor. ''And birthdays and holidays.''

''What about me?'' He shocked himself a whole lot more than he surprised her.

"You?" She did a creditable job of laughing heartily even as the wave of sensation swamped her caused by such a thought. She even managed not to wait too long before she added, "You're not looking," hoping he would deny it.

"That's true." But his tongue wouldn't leave the subject. He said, "You might consider me. I could fill the qualifying parts of impregnating, support and holidays."

More slowly, in words drenched with longing, she replied, "We're totally unsuited. Ah, there's the timer for the eggs."

With her escape into the kitchen, their strange hypothesis was ended. He began to castigate himself for ever blurting any of it, for now he could not possibly kiss her good-night. If he tried to kiss her now, she would think his suggestion to consider him as a candidate to father her children had been serious, and she'd back off as if stung by a hornet.

His genetic obsession with redheads had betrayed him, and the very thought of possessing her had totally ruined his usual practical control. Now what was he supposed to do? He didn't want marriage, he reminded himself. He only wanted to bed her.

He was going to have to pull back and try to mend the fragile beginning of cordial friendship until she lowered her guard again. Just watch, she'd be back to calling him Mr. Blake, but there was no way he was going to call her Miss Moore. About the only thing that would help him was if Phil should make a real try and he could rescue her. Fat chance.

With cold water running over the pan of cooked eggs, Sarah appeared to exactly follow his thoughts. "I believe your entire evening was wasted. I'm paranoid about Phil. He's right down there with big spiders and snakes, but the phone hasn't even rung."

"He's outside in his car, waiting for you to come home."

"Don't terrify me."

"Are you that afraid of him?"

"I would never have gone to the office alone with him to hunt files on a Sunday evening."

"Even knowing judo?"

"He doesn't fight fair."

"But I would?" He watched her with an easy look. He didn't feel at all like playing fair in a struggle for her.

"You're not interested." She appeared blithely sure.

He was so shocked by her assurance that he didn't move or reply. She didn't realize the extent of her impact on him? How could she be so obtuse?

She waited for his reply without breathing, knowing full well he had no interest in her whatsoever. She wanted him to say he was on fire for her, that he couldn't go another minute without holding her body against his and driving her so berserk she'd match his own madness. He didn't say a word. He thought of her as a rag, a bone, and a hank of hair. He probably even had the ancient British superstition about redheads being bad luck.

They stood there as if frozen in time. Finally she said, "Thank you very much for your support this evening. You were brilliant. Do you lead a devious life that you can be clever about cars and lights?" She smiled a little sadly.

He ignored her question. "You're without a car. I'll come by for you in the morning. What time's the picnic?"

"Not until ten. We can call one of the others to come by for us or take a cab to the garage. There's no need for you to bother."

"No bother. I'll be here about nine-thirty, will that be all right?"

"Will you be going to the picnic?" Her smile brightened.

"I was invited when it was planned here at your party last week."

"Of course." But she looked at him, wondering why he would go if he wasn't in the market for a wife. He was using this opportunity as so many males did. He wanted to look over the field of available women. Her smile dimmed down to almost nothing.

They went to her side door between the two big houses where there was a minute porch. It was his idea to slip out and go over to his car without appearing to have come from her house.

"Did you make your first fortune as a cat burglar?" She didn't actually know one thing about him—only that her body wanted his.

"Be sure not to turn on any other lights before you go to bed."

"I won't."

"Good night. I'll see you about nine-thirty." He didn't kiss her. It was a good thing he had already braced himself not to. All his cells were frantic for her, but if he did kiss her, they'd all come unglued.

Still in one vibrating mass, he went soundlessly down the side stairs and disappeared into the night.

Six

In spite of Joan sleeping in the spare bedroom and Lily Anna yowling away in the kitchen, Sarah's apartment seemed empty after Steven left. But he'd be back tomorrow at nine-thirty! What would she wear? She could put on chiffon and feathers and greet him at the door with one arm up along the doorjamb as she leaned there in a lax and inviting way. She'd say, "Hiii, Steeevinnnn . . ." Sure she could.

Tomorrow's outing was a picnic. What could she wear to impress Steven Blake and not look like a complete idiot who was dead set on attracting a man? She, who had given up men.

She went through her closet and finally faced the fact that she would have to wear something at least similar to jeans and a T-shirt or she'd attract all sorts of comments and speculation from the Possibles. Since she knew all the others too well—so well that they were like relatives and none could entice her—the speculators would soon set on Steven Blake as the object of her interest.

She did have the new jogging outfit. A red-greyed green that was dark as a forest. It made her hair quite spectacular. Perhaps she should give her hair a brown rinse. Tone it down. No, he would have to get used to the real her. And anyway, he'd already seen her hair every day for almost a month.

The jogging outfit was in the laundry, so she went to sleep to Lily Anna's yowls accompanied quite nicely by the rhythmic washer. And she dreamed. She had on a red jogging suit that clashed horribly with her hair! She struggled to remember why on earth she'd chosen *that* color! Since she had on a jogging outfit, she felt compelled to jog, and Steven couldn't keep up with her. It was maddening.

The next morning she looked a little like a Christmas tree with that red hair and green jogging suit. She sparkled. Her eyes were like blue diamonds, and at first her smile flashed but was suddenly self-consciously gone. Nevertheless she glowed.

Joan watched Sarah cautiously; she was surprised she hadn't seen this coming. Sarah was in love with Steven Blake. Joan became very quiet and scared for her. He'd break Sarah's heart. Troubadours should all be shot for singing about the glories of love. It was a false premise. Love hurt. With love one suffered... and was lonely... and insecure. Love was a bane. Husbands were constantly tempted by predatory nurses who were right at hand and willing.

All Sarah could think of was that she would have the day with Steven. She ignored the others who would be there, and thought of the picnic as just the two of them. But when he came for her—and Joan, of course—he was in a suit and tie. "What...?" She lifted a hand near her chest and pointed a finger at his tie. "Aren't you . . . ?"

He could see her disappointment! He was elated she regretted he wouldn't be going to the picnic. He was almost as exhilarated by her disappointment as he was regretful not to go. "They've called a meeting. I might get to the picnic later. You look gorgeous."

"It's just a jogging suit." She felt so sunk she felt like staying home. How could she do that now? It would look as if she wouldn't go without him, and then he'd know she was attracted to him—to Steven Blake, the confirmed bachelor. "Will you be in time for lunch?"

"I'll quit my job if they don't let me go."

Her smile came back. "I'll save you something to eat."

A tingle went down him. He looked beyond her to nod a greeting to Joan and wished he had the ability to blink and send her to some unknown place for two hours. He looked back at Sarah and decided he'd rather blink the two of them to the edge of paradise. Instead he smiled and asked, "Ready?"

She nodded gravely.

"Did the eggs come out okay? I could test them for you."

"You don't have to," she replied a bit sassily as she led him into the kitchen and displayed the plastic plate with all its molded rounds filled with deviled eggs artfully decorated with bits of parsley. "I had only enough to fill the plate."

He simply took one egg half and popped it into his mouth as if it were his right. His eyes twinkled, his face was smug, his air quite arrogant, his manner teasing.

If she hadn't liked him, been bemused by him, she would have frowned, her lips would have thinned and she would have quickly covered the plate. Instead she gasped and exclaimed, "Why, Steven! I just told you not to!" She stood there before him looking deliciously indignant. Just asking for it.

He said, "That wasn't enough to tell." And he took another. His eyes laughed down at her as he chewed.

She scolded, "Now what am I supposed to do with the gaps? Just look at that plate. It looks . . . moth-eaten."

He said, "I'll balance it." And he took another.

"Steven!" she cried in protest.

Her mouth was almost too tempting, but Joan stood in the kitchen doorway watching them quite seriously. His eyes came back to Sarah as he asked, "Any more parsley?"

"Didn't you have breakfast?"

"No time." He turned his wrist to see his watch. "Gotta go. Hustle up, woman. How's Lily Anna this morning? Hung over?"

"He spends his mornings under the bushes in the backyard." Sarah handed him another of the eggs, scooped out a tomato and filled it with a small bouquet of parsley before she placed it in the center of the rearranged egg platter. Joan helped gather the picnic paraphernalia, and the three went out to Steven's car.

He told them goodbye at the parking garage and took off. Sarah retrieved her stored car and Joan was silent as Sarah drove out 38th Street, west of town, to Eagle Creek. After a time, and by then they were driving through the Speedway section of Indianapolis, Joan said, "You be careful. He eats little girls like you on his toast for breakfast.''

Sarah replied soberly, ''Yes.''

It scared Joan even more that Sarah didn't question what Joan was talking about and she felt compelled to add, ''He won't marry you.''

''I know.''

''Now, Sarah...''

''You've done your duty.''

Waiting at the picnic ground was Joan's tall, thin, bearded husband Luke. ''I'm free for twenty-four hours! What took you so long?'' He laughed and held out his arms. Joan stood there not believing her eyes, then she walked into his arms and just lay her head on his chest while he talked to everyone else.

A hammock had been rigged between two trees for Luke and he was fed an early lunch. He slept the rest of the day while Joan smiled.

Sarah worried that he was sleeping too long and said to Joan, ''He'll be up all night!'' As soon as the words were out of her mouth, she laughed and wasn't surprised when Joan replied, ''Yes.''

Steven didn't arrive until just after two. Sarah had almost given up hope. But his car wheeled in and she saw him stride toward them carrying sweatpants, shirt and running shoes. Their eyes met across the distance and they laughed. Sarah's throaty laugh alerted the rest and there was the silence of intense curiosity as Steven approached the group. This was a man who interested Sarah Moore.

She almost got up to go to meet him, but stopped herself both times, before finally rising and moving toward him. All this was noted by the rest as it was unusual behavior for Sarah.

Curiosity was the prime response of the group. True, there was some protectiveness, for they were all fond of Sarah to varying degrees. In some there was a little jealousy, but the overwhelming sentiment was curiosity about a man who—at last—could interest Sarah Moore.

Like any man, Steven was conscious of the others. He was the stranger. He automatically gauged the male reaction to his intrusion. With some surprise he noted that more than half the group of roughly forty people were men. They were all about thirty years old, though some were noticeably younger or older. He registered all that but his eyes kept coming back to Sarah. Did she realize that her eyes were openly welcoming? He grinned at her as he wondered if she thought there were shorted-out wires under the ground. Was her body tingling? His sure as hell was.

"How was your meeting?" She burst into conversation to avoid throwing herself into his arms. He was *there*!

"Very interesting. I made them work through lunch. Did you save me anything?"

And one of the men, Jim, said, "Don't eat too much. We're choosing up sides for baseball. Will you play?"

"I'll fit in anywhere." He grinned down at Sarah. "Any more eggs?"

"I saved you two. And some fried chicken? Roast-beef sandwich? Mattie brought a chocolate pie that's sinful."

"Lead me to it."

"Change in the rest rooms over there, and it'll be ready for you."

"How serious is the baseball?" he asked as they walked away from the others to the tables still set up.

"It varies with the people. Some take it grimly and others find it hilarious."

"Half a roast-beef sandwich and a beer. Okay? I'll eat the rest later."

"All right." She smiled shyly and with such gladness. He was there.

When he returned, dressed in the sweatpants and shirt and carrying his suit Joan was standing with Sarah. Joan indicated her sleeping husband and said, "Steven, I'd like you to meet my husband, Luke."

Softly Steven told the sleeping man, "How do you do? Quite well, from the look of it." He grinned at Joan, who went off to the rough baseball diamond.

So the pair was alone. Sarah was exquisitely conscious of their isolation as a couple. She used her role as hostess as justification for being with Steven. It was her place to be cordial and kind to a newcomer whom she knew better than the rest. She wasn't fooled by her reasoning. She was there because she wanted to be with him.

He said, "The meeting was *really* interesting. I'll be able to tell you all about it in a couple of days. Interesting." He shook his head as he chewed. And again he said it: "Interesting."

"You've fired my curiosity."

"I don't believe you'll be surprised."

"Good heavens! How could you tease me so?"

They sat next to each other at a table while he held a portion of sandwich in one hand and the can of beer in the other. How unthreatening. Then he slowly swung his head to look at her. His look stabbed her with such sexual intensity that she almost reeled. She realized he wanted her as badly as she craved him! That sobered her. While she had thought she was wallowing in an unrequited passionate longing, he was far ahead of her planned flirtatious beginnings with his willingness to more than fulfill all her desires.

"Hurry up, Steve!" Voices called to them. "We need you in right field."

"Coming!" He stood, still chewing. "You playing?" His eyes challenged.

Was he being subtle? "They let me keep score." She was cautious.

"I'll give you lessons," he promised, although he didn't say in what. He jogged effortlessly over to their diamond and caught up a glove to go out to right field. He ended up playing first base brilliantly. He played easily, and enjoyed it. They made him bat left-handed because he was that good, and he slid into second and scraped his elbow and hip on the rough ground. His side won. He teased and catcalled and made even grudging ones like him.

Steven was funny. He was so skilled at playing ball that he could clown, and he had them in stitches. No one knew that he'd really hurt himself when he slid because he made such a funny issue of it. But Sarah knew, and her own body felt the sting of the strawberry hurt as if it were her own. She had to see to it, and when she did, she could put her hand on his skin. "It has to be scrubbed," she told him seriously.

He looked down at her and his eyes were hidden by his lashes as he smiled. "All right."

All the ways and places she wanted to scrub him zipped through her mind, and when they slowed down for selected replays, her knees became unreliable.

There are men who are made to be leaders. They can go in and take control and lead. This can be done in a variety of ways: with power, threats, inspiring awe, or with skill of personality. Steven's incredible talent lay in being not only physically dexterous, but knowing how to be likable. He was so natural. No one knew his was deliberate. It was his field. He did it automatically. He wanted Sarah, if only for a while. To get her, he had to be friends with her friends. If he never saw any of them again, he'd never miss them. They would remember him fondly, but he would no longer need them, for by then he would have had Sarah.

But Phil had come to the picnic. Wearing casual clothes that were too expensive to risk damage from any exertion, he sat talking and was apparently accepted by everyone. Although Sarah shunned him, there were women who welcomed him, and men who accepted him quite readily. Steven found himself unable to exert his natural affability. For the first time in his life he felt an odd, instinctive hostility toward another man. He'd felt competitive before but had never experienced this strange pagan antagonism. He wanted to rip Phil's gullet and remove his gizzard with his bare hands. That sobered Steven. A friendly man opposes violence on general principle. Why should he feel that way about a man Sarah didn't even like? Phil was no threat to his designs on Sarah. So what was the problem?

With the game over, Steven lay back on the ground and allowed Sarah to wait on him. He did that to annoy Phil, and it worked. Phil asked Sarah, "Where did you go last night? I went past your place and your car wasn't there."

"It was at the garage," she replied without looking at Phil.

"But you were home?"

"Of course." She gave him an icy look.

"Sorry I missed you."

She couldn't think of a good reply and so was silent.

Steven asked, "Any more of the ham?"

She was contrite. "It's all gone. But there's another piece of chicken. Would you like that?"

He smiled at Sarah and his eyes slid over to Phil. All Phil had to do was listen to Sarah's words and tone to know whom she wanted. She wanted him! He said softly, "I've had enough. I could use one more of your eggs, but I polished those off first. Come sit by me." His voice was low and seductively commanding as he patted the ground by him.

He almost expected her to refuse, and he was prepared to tease her for being afraid of him, but she came and sat—not close or intimately—but nearby in the group. Several had brought guitars, which they started playing. They joined in to sing the songs of their college days, the peace songs, the songs of troubled times. Songs of conscience, songs of nostalgia.

During that session Luke wakened, refreshed. He was starved, and Joan fed him. Neither woman was aware how similarly they served their men, but the men knew and they exchanged a communicating glance.

And Steven appeared to have one beer too many. He stood a bit unsteadily, his eyelids almost closed and he smiled. He was a hilarious drunk. He told stories and laughed, and he listened and laughed. He was rolling drunk...and he couldn't drive home. Sarah laughed with him as she gathered his clothing and shoes, and she told the others, "I know where he lives; I'll drive him. Will someone take my car?"

Joan and Luke volunteered as Phil asked Sarah, "How will you get home?"

"No problem." Sarah didn't want to talk to Phil.

"I'll follow you." Phil was firm.

"No need."

"It's no trouble." Phil was adamant. "I'll do it."

Sarah said coldly, "No."

Steven corrected a slight list to port and put in, "Bug off, buster." But he sputtered over "buster" and had to work on the word. His struggles with the pronunciation made the others laugh so hard that they quite cheerfully interfered for him and told Phil to leave Sarah alone. When she started Steven's car, the others easily blocked Phil from following.

As Sarah drove along, Steven sprawled on the passenger seat, one arm along the window-sill and one flung up over the seat back. He sang. He had a good voice. He sang sea chanties that were hummed here and there as he laughed that infectious laugh. She told him, "You sing better than Lily Anna."

He told her in a low, male-to-female, teasing voice, "I have other attributes which Lily Anna lacks."

He *was* drunk. What outrageous things would he say? She replied with a quelling, "Oh?" wanting to hear him, yet not wanting to appear to encourage him.

He said, "I have a male . . . name."

She laughed in spite of herself.

He went on, "And, unlike Lily Anna, I am potentially dangerous to a female. Specifically to any redheaded woman close by." He turned his head, chin first, and looked down his nose at her as he gave her a smug, wicked look.

He was harmless, she knew that; he couldn't even say buster! She pretended a diligent attentiveness to the traffic and did not reply. She was a little flustered. Not only by his words. There was something not...quite...right. But her body was too aware of his for her mind to pay close attention. In her mind she was trying to sort out exactly what caused the sound of a larger alarm bell than the ordinary, everyday ones that rang when she might be in danger.

When at last they arrived at his apartment it was evening. The spring weather was fine, and

the day ending. It was calm and pretty with
new leaves and spring's flowers of tulips, jon-
quils, hyacinths, and daffodils. She waited, but
he just sat in the car, looking peaceful and
quiet. She got out on her side and went around
and opened his door.

His eyes almost closed, he questioned, "We
there?"

"Come on. On your feet. I can't carry you."

Quite firmly he said, "I don't need any help
at all." He heaved himself from the car to suddenly cling to the door, then he leaned over
along the roof of the car and bragged, "Made
it."

She was still holding his keys. She lifted them
and rattled them a little as she said, "I'll go
open the door." She went off and up the stairs
to his apartment where she unlocked the door
and left it open. He didn't follow so she went
back downstairs and looked out the front door
of the complex. He was standing there by the
car, his arms spread wide on its roof, as he
looked off into the evening's sunset and he
sang of life on the ocean. His soft, low voice
had true pitch. It was really moving—men
singing moved her soul. She went to him.

He smiled sweetly, his eyes slits, and said, "Well, hello there, honey. Are you a mermaid?"

She looked around and, as is always the case when someone is needed, there was no one else around. She said, "Come on. I'll help you to your door."

"I don't need any help." He told her amicably, and he started off, but his list was carrying him off to starboard.

Sarah closed the car door and hurried after him, putting his arm around her shoulder and hers about his waist.

"I like friendly women." He beamed down at her.

"I'm not that friendly."

"Of course not." He shook his head a little too far and stumbled, but he caught himself nicely, and she moved on. He had to stop and expound on the tulips. She kept watching for some male to help her, but no one came outside. She urged him on toward his apartment.

"What did you have in mind?" he inquired with stilted care to his tongue.

"I need to get you inside because if I leave you here, it will get quite cool tonight, and you might chill."

"You're very kind." He put both arms around her and hugged her as he sagged unsteadily. He never actually put much weight on her. He appeared to stagger, but he never floundered out of control.

They finally arrived at his door and she said, "I hope you feel okay in the morning."

"I'll go out and sleep under the bushes in your backyard with Lily Anna."

She chuckled. "Take care."

He said solemnly. "You promised to clean my arm and side where I slid into second."

She became uncertain. "Can't you do it yourself?"

He appeared to make a concerted effort to find his side. "I think so."

The abrasions should be washed. She said, "Can you get out of your clothes by yourself?"

"Anytime," he assured her quite firmly.

"Well... You do that and I'll turn on the shower for you. Can you stand under the shower okay?"

"I probably need you to hold me." But he smiled just a little.

She told him bracingly, "I'm sure you'll be perfectly all right."

He didn't reply but began to fumble in concentration on his drawstring. She fled into the bath to turn on the shower and lay out towels. She started back to tell him the shower was ready whenever he could manage, but she met him in the doorway and he was already gloriously naked.

She took a quick breath as an almost crippling sensation shot through her. He smiled, saying, "Pardon me, sir," and stepped back from the doorway to give her room to pass. He finally took her arm and helped her by him before he went on carefully into the bath and closed the door.

She put both hands to her head to keep it from floating away, then took deep breaths as she listened to him singing in the shower—another chant, in another language. She found the linen closet and took a sheet out to lay it on the unmade bed, then in the kitchen she found a towel, a bowl and soap. She figured if she just got the scrapes clean, he could put medication on the roughened "strawberry" skin the next day.

He was in the shower for a long time. She tapped on the door, but he couldn't hear her over his singing, and she had to enter, go over to the shower curtain and say, "You've really been in there long enough."

He ripped the curtain aside and grinned at her. "Come on in! The water's great!"

He was magnificent! She faltered and replied, "I need to see your side..."

So he turned to her! She quickly put the curtain back in place, and he laughed a very low and amused chuckle. That big bell boomed again in her warning system. She tried to think if that particular one had ever sounded before in all her twenty-nine years? It had to be her last-gasp defense system and therefore very serious. For her own sake, she should get out of Steven's apartment right now. But how could she leave him until he was safely in bed? Drunk, he could fall, or go to sleep on his back and choke. No, she had to see him safely into bed.

To the deep boom of the biggest bell, she held a towel for Steven. He turned off the shower and stepped from the tub. She closed her eyes. He leaned and kissed her cheek, and water dripped from his hair onto her. He smelled delicious. She heard the sounds of him drying himself. In a breathless, tiny voice she said, "Put the towel around you."

"Okay." He said that as he moved on past her.

She thought "Darn!" then opened her eyes and turned to watch him go out of the bathroom and saw the towel was around his shoulders!

He saw the bowl by the bed and the sheet for him to lie on. He dropped his towel, lay down and stretched out with a big sigh. And a smile. She came to him and arranged the sheet more modestly. He coughed a little. She squeezed out the kitchen towel. He cautioned, "Don't tickle."

She resisted a teasing reply and said rather staunchly, "It looks pretty clean. You must have done a good job of it in the shower. I don't see any dirt at all."

"There's the unseen dirt. We ought to be . . . sure."

"Yes." She was uncertain. "I suppose so." She looked at his bare skin, marred only by the strawberry-colored abrasions. Then she took a bracing breath and gently began to wash the injured skin.

He twitched a couple of times and she made sympathetic sounds in her throat. He said softly, "Stay with me."

"No. You've had too much to drink."

"I'm not drunk."

Scoffing, she commanded, "Say 'buster.'"

He turned slowly to his back and said perfectly, "Buster." He smiled as he opened his eyes and looked at her. His eyes weren't drunkenly bloodshot but soberly clear, and very amused.

In that instant she realized he'd been speaking quite clearly since they'd gotten in the car! *That* was why the big bell had been booming its warning in her mind! She exclaimed, "Why Steven, you're a sham!"

"Yes." He smiled. Then he added quite reasonably, "How else was I to get you inside my apartment to give me a bath?"

Seven

Her face blank, Sarah straightened woodenly. "You fooled us all."

Steven explained quite seriously, "Playing drunk is a very difficult thing to do realistically. Most people overplay. The whole trick is to be subtle and pretend . . . not that you're out of control but carefully in control."

"Do you do this often?" She was rather stony faced.

"I did a study of it. Pretending to be a little to the wind is sometimes a smart thing to do at a martini luncheon. It puts people at their ease. They think they're in control and you're not too swift. You have no idea how tricky people can be!''

"You can say that? You! A man who fooled us all deliberately into thinking he was incapable of driving?''

"All for a good cause." He rolled up easily from the bed but she stepped back.

"Keep your distance!''

"Now, Sarah, you know you want to be here." He paused and smiled at her. He was so unaware of his marvelous nakedness.

She was acutely aware. She backed up another step. It was only a half step but she said accusingly, "You are too calculating.''

That interested him. "Should I have kept it secret and simply overwhelmed you? You would have been willing. You know it. You do want me.''

She did. She said, "I'm not sure.''

With his smile so normal, he held out an unthreatening hand and darned if she didn't put hers into it before she even considered what she was doing. She'd been distracted by the deep booming of the big bell reverberating inside her skull.

Her hand trembled in his. That excited him in a strange way he'd never experienced. He lifted her hand to lay it on his hot chest before he slid his hand down her arm to curl around her shoulder to draw her to him as his other hand helped on her opposite side at her waist. His voice husky, he whispered urgently, "Sarah..." as his head moved down so his mouth could find hers.

Inside his hairy chest, and under her palm, she could feel his heart thudding rapidly. She became aware his breathing was disturbed. But then his mouth closed over hers and she was lost in her own body's reaction to him. She gasped at the last possible minute as her defenses scrambled and her mouth surrendered to his.

Her one small hand was braced quite ineffectively against his chest. It was her only bit of resistance, like a final brave soldier against an onslaught. But he only took her hand and put it on the back of his head, where it stayed meekly there.

When he lifted his mouth to suck in a ragged breath, she said "Steven . . ." very faintly.

His voice shook as he said, "My God, I've wanted to kiss you that way since I first saw you in the parking lot, extricating your coat from your car door."

"My coat?" She wasn't clicking too well.

"You'd locked your door on your coat." But then he went back to the business at hand. His arms crushed her to him, leaving her breathless and a little faint, while he kissed her silly.

When he moved his hands he inadvertently allowed her to breathe, and she leaned her head back and put her hands on his ears to fondle them. Her eyes didn't focus and she said, "You're so strong." That *is* what she said? Surely not. Her own ears couldn't believe it and strained for a rebuttal.

He replied, "You have on too many clothes."

She hadn't noticed that. She said "Oh?" in some surprise. Her face was briefly covered as he pulled off her top but she looked up in time to see it arch away in the air as if by magic. He unsnapped her bra and pulled the straps forward so they slid down off her arms. He breathed in quickly, then pulled her very close to him again, and he groaned as if in dreadful pain. For the first time in her life she felt the erotic sensation of a male chest against her bare, tender breasts.

She pressed herself closer, and her hands went to his sides and then around to his back to slide over the taut muscles under his smooth flesh. She said, "Oh, Steven..." and forgot whatever it was she was going to mention.

He was trembling by then. Shivering. He had never in his life been so taken by such a storm of desire. It was her red hair. Fleetingly, he wondered if his genetic contributor had ever experienced an actual redhead. Actual...?

Quite slowly, he peeled off her jogging pants and the practical cotton briefs. Her skin was alabaster all over, and her decoration was indeed red. She was glorious. Amazing. Gorgeous. He kissed her. Then he rose and held her to him. "Sarah," he said tenderly.

As his passion grew his hands were a little rougher on her and his mouth more demanding. She was swept along into his maelstrom rather fearfully, and she squeaked and gasped and wasn't sure of what she was doing. He was.

He tore the extra sheet off the bed and it joined her clothing on the floor. The bed was a ready nest, and he laid her in it. He joined her, making sweet love to her, crooning to her, telling her she was beautiful to his eyes...to his hands, to his mouth, and...to his body. He hesitated only briefly—and felt her falter—but nothing could stop him by then. He lost track of everything else except her and his vortex of pleasure. But he went alone down that last free-fall to enchantment.

He lay on her, his sweat making them slippery, and he panted from his exertions. His hands were still unsteady as he patted her head, his mouth was soft and undemanding now as he sipped kisses on her shoulder, her throat, and along her jaw. He tasted tears. "Are you all right?"

"Amazed."

He lifted from her, to lie beside her, and his big hand moved on her stomach. "Amazed?"

"What a lot of work! I don't believe I realized it took so much...effort."

"I was a little excited." His self-deprecating rumble was low and amused. He'd never been so out of control! And though replete, he longed to take her again. What if she was addictive? His father had warned him about redheads. He smiled down at her lively eyes and rubbed her stomach and petted the red frill that validated her hair. "You are fantastic," he told her. He watched his brown hand on her alabaster skin and he almost shook his head once. "You're a miracle of beauty. And how did you last so long without some man making love to you before this?"

"I was never interested."

"But I interest you?" He was quite smug.

"Well, since I've given up men."

He laughed so that he had to lean back on the other pillow. He finally turned laughing eyes to her and questioned, "In this particular position you can say you've 'given up' men?"

"Well, yes. If I was still in the market for a husband, you would never have managed to get me into bed."

"I'm sure that makes complete sense."

"Naturally," she agreed. Then she said, "I'm a little disappointed."

That caught his attention. "What do you mean?"

"I had understood it was exciting for women too. Obviously you were having a terrific time, to judge from all the noise and uh, the concentrated attention; but while it was very nice, and very pleasurable, I'm not sure it was worthwhile."

"Oh, it was!" he hastened to assure her. "Very." Then he tousled her red hair and added, "Give me a little while and I'll have you dancing. I just didn't know you needed some extra time."

"Have you had a staggering number of women?" she asked chattily.

"Ladies never ask that!" he chided.

"I don't believe I've ever had the opportunity before, and since you don't count, I thought I could inquire. I know nothing about men, really. Have you?"

He . . . didn't count? What did she mean by that? But he couldn't bring himself to ask. He replied, "Perhaps I read a lot."

She burst into a bubble of laughter. "You want to imply you were a virgin?"

"What would be so unusual about that? You were."

"I know. But I'm a woman. Men don't pay too much attention to such things."

"Oh, yes." He disagreed quite seriously. "I'm honored you allowed me to love you."

"Well, it is certainly interesting. I've never felt such strange sensations. Your hands do very odd things to me . . . inside me. And your mouth . . ."

"Like this?" He moved his evening's whiskers down her throat very gently.

She gasped, "Oh, my . . ." But she stopped.

He lifted his head. "Oh, your . . . what?"

"I don't suppose I should say, 'Oh my goodness!' under these circumstances." Her blue eyes danced.

"Do you like that?"

"Extremely."

"I have other . . . things I've read about that women like."

"Tell me."

"I believe it will be more informative if I . . . show you." He did. Exquisitely. He showed her until she danced right over the edge of forever and glimpsed paradise.

* * *

They napped for awhile, then lay awake and talked. She said, "I've never spent a night with a man before."

"See? I'm trying to expand your sensibilities with unique experiences! And anyway, I'm glad you're here, so Phil couldn't get his nasty hands on you."

With the dismissiveness of someone who feels very secure, she scoffed, "Phil!"

He made her giggle, which he thought sounded like music. And she inquired as to why he'd asked her not to tickle him. "Are you ticklish?"

He denied it.

She instructed, "That really isn't something one can be sure about. I would be glad to give you a test."

He considered that profoundly but said, "Although I appreciate your interest in scientific research, you must recall I've been grievously wounded in the fray." Then he had the audacity to add, "And it's the wrong time of the month." He made her laugh.

They explored and tasted. She laughed the laugh of a woman who is teasing a man deliciously and knows it. He allowed her to do that. Eventually they got up and went through his refrigerator but it didn't offer much choice in food. They had a simple omelet, tea, and graham crackers.

"I haven't had a graham cracker in fifteen years!" she exclaimed.

"They're a secret lust of mine."

"We all have our Achilles' heel."

"Well . . . ?" He encouraged her confidence. "You know mine."

She tilted her head back a little, her red hair in disarray, as she sat there in his robe, her cheeks red from his whiskers, and her blue eyes looked languorous. "I believe—" she hesitated "—I believe I've found a new vice."

He whooped laughter, picked her up and carried her back to the bedroom. But he warned, "You keep this up and the next time you'll have to carry me!"

She smiled a Mona Lisa smile, but he kissed her quite hungrily and no more was said.

When morning came again, and they lay in bed recovering, he said, "I don't understand why, with you, I can't be satisfied. You take me to paradise, but I still want you."

"Not right now. I have to wash my hair."

"I'll do it for you."

"You rest up." She crawled off the bed and he lay lax, watching. A marvelous, soft smile lit his face. He still didn't know what had happened to him.

Later, as they again sat at the kitchen table, they talked of many things. She asked him, "Where did you learn the songs of the sea?"

"I spent several summers, when I was... oh... sixteen to about nineteen, crewing a masted racing ship. There were nine of us and they worked our tails off. Everything was done by hand. The chants give rhythm to movement, and therefore we all pull at once and get things done, because the chant makes us pull together. The song is also good for morale. You learn the words almost by osmosis. The chant I was singing last night in the shower was to Poseidon for my Lorelei to come to me." He smiled quietly at her. "I never knew it worked."

"A Lorelei was a siren who sat on the rocks in the Rhine River and lured sailors to wreck their ships."

He nodded. "I feel reasonably wrecked."

Suddenly she exclaimed, "Good Heavens! I didn't give Lily Anna his rum last night! You have no idea how irascible he is when he hasn't had his rum."

"He can't have two slugs in one day." Steven was reasonable.

"Half now and half later. Mrs. Thompson trusted me!"

"Who is more important? Lily Anna or me?"

"Lily Anna has only the rum. You are more fortunate."

"Yes."

At Sarah's house, they found the Parkingtons had delivered her car. Lily Anna received his jot of rum out the back door so he couldn't sink his testy claws into Sarah's alabaster ankles. But then Steven growled and snarled into her throat and dug his fingers into her here and there, and to placate *his* disposition, she led him into her bedroom as she laughed at him...

But her bedroom had been trashed! The window was broken, the bed torn apart, and all her clothes were out of drawers and closets. The couple looked at the mess, then looked at each other.

The police came, examined everything and wrote a complete description. None of the neighbors had heard or seen anything. Steven made some calls. Sarah was rigid with anger. She wasn't particularly afraid for she thought Phil was probably responsible. It was something he might do because she had spurned him.

None of her clothing had been ripped and there was nothing written on the walls. She couldn't find that anything was missing. The mess could be the result of Phil's brief temper. Her car was there, she wasn't, where was she? But it was still a broken window, intrusion; and the clothes had to be washed and put away. It repulsed her to think of anyone else's hands on her things.

After the police left, with assurances they'd be keeping an eye on her place, she put the first run of clothes in the washer. Steven told her, "You'll stay with me."

"Don't be ridiculous!"

"I will not have you here alone."

"There'll be no danger."

"Then I'm staying here. I'll go get some things."

"Steven!"

"Again? You can't always be nagging me into bed, honey, there *are* other things in li—"

She laughed. He watched her laugh and thought how different her reactions were to most women's. All the responses she might have made to his protest—from indignation to pouting, to embarrassment, to sly preening—but Sarah had laughed. He grinned and went to kiss her cheek and pat her bottom in the way men do with women who attract them. But when he turned to leave, taking his car keys from his pocket, she said quite adamantly, "You may *not* live here. We work in the same office. We would be a terrible scandal! I won't have it."

He looked at the ceiling and put a hand to his forehead in an elaborate display of tried patience and said, "Small towns are a bore."

"There are almost a million people in Indianapolis."

"Like New York City, it's basically a small town."

"You're impossible!" She laughed.

"It's true. There's no place on earth as provincial as New York City. The people there believe they are the center of all culture and need nothing more, and they pity anyone who can't live there. How more closed can anyone be? Petersburg, Illinois, is more open-minded.''

''Even Petersburg would frown on our living together.''

He sighed. ''Yes.''

''New York wouldn't.''

He was forced to agree. ''But only because they would think we were doubling up to save on rent. Rents are shocking in New York City.''

''They are in Indianapolis.''

''And even in Petersburg.''

''But it's working together that blows this one,'' she explained. ''We must not. Everyone would think I was trying to climb the corporate ladder on my back.''

''I didn't know you were ambitious.''

''Since I'm not going to marry, I need to secure my future. I had planned to go into the Peace Corps, but I do need a little backlog of cash before I do anything so rash as taking a sabbatical. I've put in a lot of years at Michaels Inc. and I can't risk my place by having a blatant affair with you.''

''I'll see to it that no one knows.''

"Look, Steven, you innocent. While the neighbors won't hear a broken window or a house trashed, they can hear a sigh or an inaudible click of a door closing. It is a phenomenal fact. Within the time it takes for you to drive back here, everyone will be at their windows, watching you carrying in a box... Surely you would be smarter than to try to actually bring in a suitcase?"

"How did you get so wise?" His tone was as if he'd confronted a guru on a mountaintop.

"All these years of eating in the company cafeteria and listening. The only thing that's saved me, in being promoted periodically by Mr. Taylor, is the fact that he is happily married, and he was so seldom around the office. If he'd been a diligent officer in the company, there would have been speculation about me."

"How can I protect you?" He frowned at her.

"The window will be repaired. I'll have all sorts of little things lined up on all the sills, and the doors are all protected with good dead bolts. If anything crashes off a windowsill, I'll be out of this house like a shot."

"To go...where?"

She revised her plans. "I'll turn on all the lights and call the police."

"That's better." He glowered at the broken window. "I suggest we change apartments. If you won't stay with me, or let me stay with you, then we'll switch." He smiled a snarling smile. "Think how surprised...someone would be! Coming through a window, in search of a delicious redhead, and finding Steven Blake instead." He gave a really nasty chuckle.

"I'll go stay with my parents."

He watched her silently. After a while he reluctantly agreed, "I think that might be the solution. I can't talk you into staying with me?"

"No."

"It ought not to be for long."

"I dislike telling my parents that someone broke into my place. They are quite protective."

"I believe that's a trait most parents share."

"I know judo." She put that in comfortably.

"Yes. I've heard that mentioned. But any woman who is afraid of a machine can't be too much of a threat to an invading man."

"I can control men. It's machines that are unreliable."

"You can control men?"

"No problem."

"Are you controlling me?"

"Of course." She lifted her nose a little and gave him a controlling look.

"You stayed with me last night."

She agreed. "I was curious."

He laughed immoderately. "You imply it was all your idea?" He laughed some more—heartily.

She smiled sweetly. "I chose to drive you home."

His attention was caught. "You ... intended to seduce me?"

"I had all the excuses: you weren't in full control, I would be washing your wounded body and could get you out of your clothes, and ... then I'd take it from there." She smiled nicely.

"It was my idea!" He touched his thumb to his chest.

She looked down modestly and her smile was quite nicely at the "slight" setting. "Of course."

"Why, Sarah Moore!" His tone was scandalized.

"Well, I was curious!" She defended herself, raising her eyes and looking misunderstood.

"We could have both saved a lot of time if you'd thought to mention it to me."

"I rather enjoyed it the way it turned out."

"So did I."

"Thanks for bringing me home. I'll see you tomorrow."

"Today's only just started. What do you mean, you'll see me tomorrow?"

"I have to get my clothes back in order, pack, and think of some reason to go stay with my folks. It's going to have to be a fairly logical reason."

"Painters?" he offered.

"Too soon." She frowned nicely. "My parents have dogs. What about Lily Anna? Want to take him home with you?"

"I have no burning desire to live with Lily Anna, however I could come here to feed him. I'd rather do that than have you over here. I'll need a key."

She found a spare and handed it to him. "Thank you."

"Are you going to kiss me goodbye?"

"Only a little one. You are extremely susceptible."

"It's genetic."

"Sex is genetic?" she questioned.

"In my family sex goes all the way back through time." He was solemn.

She grinned at him. "We do it by osmosis. It's neater."

"Not anymore, you don't."

They kissed. And again. And again. She squirmed away while she still could. "Goodbye."

It annoyed him that she had been the one to send him off. To leave was his male prerogative. She should be clinging to him and begging him to stay.

He still didn't understand last night's comment when she said he didn't count. She did like him. Her eyes said so. Her body was positive. How could she now send him off so easily? What was she going to do that he couldn't be around?

*   *   *

Sarah strained her big-bell-damaged brain to come up with a plausible reason for going to stay with her parents. If worse came to worst she could tell the truth, but she really hated to worry them. The intruder was more than likely Phil. He was a known quantity and wouldn't actually harm her. But messing up her room was unusual behavior even for him. It was a little tilted. He might be more dangerous than she suspected. She would need to be careful.

She packed a suitcase and looked around. Lily Anna was sitting outside the window on the ledge looking inside. She went over and told him to behave. He switched his tail in temper. She looked around some more; picked up her needlepoint, her address book, her calendar, and a couple of books. Then she left.

She found her parents bustling around. Unusually agitated, her mother said, "Your phone must be out of order. We've been trying to get in touch since last night!"

"What's going on?"

"If you didn't hear the tape, why did you bring a suitcase? We need you to stay here while we're gone."

"Gone where?"

"Your Aunt Ditty fell down the stairs, we've got to go right away. All is chaos. With the kids and all." She spoke to Sarah, her husband and herself in the same hodgepodge. "I'm taking my own skillet. And that spoon. I can't cook without them. She needs me. See to the plants, and the dogs, I'm so glad you're here. This is a mess. Hurry. We were going to leave a note." And still talking in that manner, her mother went out to the car with Sarah trailing along. Her dad smiled and kissed her cheek. "Don't worry," he assured her, "we'll be back in time for the scout trip." Then he got into the car too and they left Sarah alone. She was where she needed to be and she'd never had to make up an excuse. She and the dogs exchanged looks, and then they all went about their own business.

Eight

Sarah wasn't sure how Steven would act toward her on Monday, but she didn't expect him to treat her ordinarily. At first she thought how smart it was of him to be so cool and in control. Then she felt irritated because *she* wasn't cool and in control. It took all her willpower not to languish or to try to distract and tempt. Then she wondered if the reason he could be so businesslike was that he'd had affairs with all his other secretaries. *That made her mad.*

Altogether it was a hell of a day. A bearcat. Mondays were always the tar pits, but this Monday was especially nasty. After the ten o'clock break she said sourly to Joan, "That does it! I'm going to quit, get married to some indifferent man and have lots of children." Joan laughed and went out of Sarah's office.

When Sarah went into Steven's office, she was startled that Steven inquired, "Lots of children from an *indifferent* man?"

Obviously he'd been eavesdropping. "Yes!" she snapped.

"I have friends with children and they drive the parents mad."

"I like kids."

"Why?"

"Have you ever seen a little kid watch *Sesame Street*?"

"No, as a matter of fact, I haven't." His face wore the polite expression of one speaking another language. "Somehow that's never been on my agenda."

She picked up the letters as he signed them. And he looked up with the last one. "How did you sleep last night?" His voice was smoky with innuendo.

"With two dogs." She gave him a cool look. "Two instead of one."

"I slept like a log. You wore me out."

She huffed in shock. "Why, Mr. Blake!" she said, turning to leave. He then got to watch her walk, but it was away from him.

At one o'clock that afternoon he asked, "You'll come to my place . . . for supper?"

"The Possibles meet tonight instead of tomorrow."

"You'd give me up for a bunch of women?"

"After you take off, buster—" she drew out that word so it was distinct "—the women will still be here."

"You're just a tad testy today. I believe it's something that can be fixed."

She thought so too, but she gave him a cool look and left him again.

He was in a meeting when she left right after five. She had delayed leaving but not in order to see Steven; it was only so she could make sure her desk was pristine.

On Tuesday Steven was already in the office when she arrived. He greeted her crossly. "Did you stay at your parents' house?"

A little surprised by his antagonism she replied briefly, "Yes."

"Why didn't you answer the phone?"

"Did you need another file?"

"What?"

"That's why you've needed to get in touch with me before."

He tightened his lips and looked down her as he considered how to reply without ravishing her right there on the "de-electrified" carpet. He said, "I'd have liked very much to have been able to get in touch with you last night."

"Rested up?"

He didn't know why she had to be so hostile. "Aren't you?"

"Did you feed Lily Anna?"

He looked startled. "I forgot."

She gave him a cold, condemning look and said, "I'll go feed him now."

"I'll come along."

"You have Mr. Winsom coming in ten minutes."

"Oh, hell." He glared at her. "I won't have you going over there alone."

"Then," she said with exquisite courtesy, "you should have fed the cat."

"Women!"

She bared her teeth in a "smile" and went out of the office.

He waited the time it would take her to get to her apartment, excused himself to Mr. Winsom and phoned her. She picked up the phone and said, "Hello?"

With Mr. Winsom listening, he said, "Miss Moore, this is Steven Blake, I was checking to see if the balance is correct?"

"How is dear Mr. Winsom?"

"Excellent."

"Lily Anna's cheeks were sunken in and he was so weakened from hunger, he could barely scratch my leg."

"And that was rectified?"

"He will be singing shortly."

"I believe that input was to be postponed."

"It was...from last night. He was having the DTs and a jolt of rum was needed immediately to steady him." Lily Anna yowled tentatively.

"Good luck."

Lily Anna yowled closer so Sarah must have taken the phone over by the cat. Even from across Steven's desk Mr. Winsom could hear the sound and he exclaimed, "What is that?"

So that Sarah could hear, Steven replied, "I believe one of the typists has broken a fingernail." And he replaced the phone.

When she returned to the office, she gave Steven what was supposed to be a cool look, but it melted into a laughing one as he shook his head at her and tried not to smile.

When he could find a private second he inquired, "Dinner tonight, Miss Moore?"

"I'll check my calendar, Mr. Blake."

The attraction between them mounted steadily during the rest of the day. They were so aware of one another that it was a miracle anyone could stand to be between them. Their tension generated such an arc of electricity that anyone nearby should have fried.

He managed a time to tell her he would follow her to her parents' house so they could go to dinner in his car. She nodded in sedate agreement. Then he was called down to the president's office just before five. She waited as the office emptied, and she then waited alone. She was about ready to give up and leave when she heard the hurried steps in the hall and the door was flung open.

If he'd been calm, she could have handled it. But he was harried and uncertain. "You're here!" he said as if he'd convinced himself she would be gone. Her emotional pitch rose to match his.

He kissed her as he backed her against her desk and held her with his hips. His mouth took hers deeply, and his hands went to cradle the back of her head.

Leaning against her, pressing her there, he lifted his mouth and put his arms around her to hold her tightly in his arms. He groaned with the exquisite pleasure of having her close. "I'm going to take you right here."

"You are not either!"

"I've heard desks are very erotic. How can I wait?"

"With discipline!"

"You damned redheads are sirens, every one of you!"

"We are not! It's men who are silly and uncontrolled."

"Only around redheads."

"I have a blond cousin..."

"Another mania altogether."

By then her blouse was free of her skirt band, one shoe was off somehow, her hair was askew, and he was wearing her lipstick. They broke apart and, breathing hard, they stared at each other. He said, "Is my hair standing on end? Everything else is."

She reached up to smooth his hair and that started the whole tussle all over again.

When next they parted just to drag in air and try to orient themselves, he said, "We need to leave here."

Leaning on both hands on her desk she nodded.

He said, "Your hair's coming down."

Her hands trembled so that she made it worse.

"Maybe you just ought to take it down."

She nodded with one hand supporting her forehead.

"You're driving me crazy."

She nodded yet again. It was easy since her head wasn't exactly on her neck but had to be a little off center.

"Somehow your blouse is out," he said.

Since her mind wasn't clicking, that made good sense. She stuffed the tail of her blouse into her skirt band but then her skirt was off center just like the rest of her.

He smoothed his tie several more times and asked, "Do I look normal?"

She focused on him after a while and she smiled. "Lipstick." She looked at her desk, then reached down and automatically opened the bottom drawer, removed a tissue and handed it to him. Having done that quite well, she began to return to reality. She looked for her shoe, and her toes put themselves inside with a practiced twist. It helped to be standing level again. She straightened her skirt, took a deep breath, and didn't risk a glance at him right then.

She took a mirror out of her purse and looked at herself. She didn't gasp, but she wiped the smeared lipstick off her face. Of course, it left what appeared to be a red streak but it was the abrasion of his evening whiskers. Then she took his advice and simply took down her hair and combed the glorious mass.

He watched mesmerized. Her hair was like a cloud of red silk. He wondered if he could ever risk showing her to his father. With his mother being so patient, and his father's blood pressure, could he? He could send a picture of Sarah to his mother, and she could pick a good day to show it to his father. That was probably better than just taking her to see them without any warning. With his dad braced—having seen Sarah's picture—maybe he could handle the real thing. If he killed off his father with Sarah, his mother might never forgive either one of them. He might have to veil her when they were around his parents. He wondered if that was why Arabs veiled their women.

"Am I all right?" she looked at him anxiously.

"You'd probably kill him."

"Mr. Effingham? Judo? Who?"

"An innocent bystander." He was satisfied with that exchange, but it left her even more confused. He took her arm and looked up and down the corridor before he took her out of their office, down the hall and out of the building. He saw her to her own car in the vacated parking lot, cautioned her to drive carefully, and to be *sure* he was following her. "Don't lose me."

She smiled blindingly.

In her mesmerized state she drove automatically to her own apartment. She was out of her car before he could get to her and ask why she was there. She hadn't a clue. But luckily Lily Anna arrived at the curb just then to mention he hadn't had supper yet and now was a good time for it. She fed him, got back in her car and drove to her parents' house. Steven was willing to stay there, but there was no way she would. "It's my *parents'* house!" She was scandalized.

"Have you any idea, just in the two hundred years since this country has been founded, how many people have made love in their parents' houses?"

She was adamant. "No."

He thought she expected him to tell her how many and he tried to judge—even roughly— how many. "Well, the population in 1776 was..."

"No, not *how many*, but—no, not here!"

"What difference does it make?" But he instantly recognized a lost cause and suggested quickly, "Let's go to my place."

She got huffy. "Is that all you want? I've had a long day. I've driven all over Indianapolis, and now all you can think about is getting me into any bed that might be handy!''

''I have never in all my adult days been this anxious or this wild for a woman. I don't recognize myself. I'm really not this clumsy. It's all your fault.''

That was a mistake. ''My fault?'' Her voice was ominously quiet.

Earnestly he put in *very quickly*, ''I was saying that to myself. 'It's all your fault.' Like that. Dumb. Let's go get ourselves an elegant meal. And some sweet music.'' Music hath charm to soothe.

And it worked. They went to the Hyatt and had a cocktail while they waited for a table down on the balcony in the dining room. He danced with her, and he did some very astute sweet-talking. She listened.

He never took his eyes off her. She knew that, because she never took hers off him. It was the only way to know something like that. If you only looked up occasionally, in between times he could be checking out the whole entire building. He didn't. He looked only at her.

Actually, he was conscious of every other male in the room and he was ready to flatten any man who came near her. There'd been two men in the lounge who'd each asked if they could dance with her. He'd looked so incredulous before he said "No" that they did understand he wouldn't allow it. The incidents had made him abnormally possessive. He still didn't really understand what had happened to him.

He didn't hurry her one jot. He talked to her. He complimented her. He shared bits of food with her, feeding them into her mouth with his fork. He smiled at her smolderingly and wasn't even aware of it. He enjoyed her. Gradually she began to flirt with him.

She wasn't a polished flirt. She was a charming amateur. She put him in thrall. His anxiety to bed her didn't diminish, but he became so bemused by her. That she was there and attending to him was another kind of lovemaking, and he relished her.

He took her to his apartment, and his lovemaking was unlike anything he'd ever experienced. Sex was *a* to *b* to *c*, and sometimes scrambled. It was variations on a theme. This time was different. It was so tender. He worshipped her. It was so wonderful. He cherished her. And then he loved her.

It was a silent loving. There was nothing to say. Or perhaps they didn't want to be distracted by thinking of speaking words. He took her clothes from her gradually, with seeming interest—not in getting her naked, but in disrobing her. When he looked at her, she blushed.

But he wasn't looking at a naked woman, he was looking at her. She couldn't be embarrassed. So then she was free to look at him and saw that he was marvelously made. So beautifully male. The shape and breadth of him, the musculature, the planes of his masculine body. She put her hands on him. His skin was so smooth over his shoulders, and so differently textured over his chest and legs.

They became known to each other, their hands smoothing and touching, their mouths tasting and kissing, as they lay there in the nest of his bed. That loving was also different. When they breathed calmly again and sighed in contentment, they smiled at each other in the darkened room.

It was midnight before he took her back to her parents' house. He didn't want to leave her, and lingered in his long good-night. Her soft, throaty laugh curled and tingled through his sated body.

"Go home," she said, locked tightly in his arms there in the entrance hall, with the dogs sitting around watching.

"Show me where you'll sleep so I can picture you there. If you don't, I'll dream of you suspended in space and I'll worry that you'll fall."

"Ohhh, nooo!" she laughed. "Go home." She didn't move.

Neither did he. "Cruel. You want me to worry about you."

"Put me there on the couch," she suggested sassily as she loosened one hand and moved it to point to the living-room couch.

"Okay."

He lifted her to walk her over to the couch with her protesting, "No, no, no, no."

He accused, "You're not going to sleep on the couch."

"I'm smart enough—in spite of the wine you've fed me *all evening long*—I'm still smart

enough not to lead you anywhere *near* a bedroom. You're susceptible.''

''You've noticed that!''

''Go home.''

He did eventually. It was after one. She
smiled as she showered and went to bed, and
she slept heavily. So did he.

The next day he put tape on the neckline of
her blouse. ''Hold still.''

''What are you doing? Steven! We're at the
office!''

''The neck of your blouse gaps.''

''It doesn't, either! I leaned over and tested
it when I bought it.''

''It gaps. I'll put some tape on it.''

''I tested it. See?'' She leaned over with her
back straight. ''It doesn't.''

''Curl your back and bring your elbows forward as if you're putting papers on my desk.''

She did and the neckline was a little scandal-
ous. ''Good heavens. It gaps!''

He smiled. ''Yes.''

''And you're only mentioning it now? I've
worn this blouse all month!''

''Well, you didn't wear it every day.''

''You could have mentioned it.''

"How?"

"There must be a tactful way for a man to warn a woman that he can see down her dress."

He laughed a marvelously amused chuckle. "I didn't mind."

"You were looking!"

"It was all right for me." He gave her the sleepy-eyed look of a sated lion who should have been surrounded by a pride of felines who protected and cared for him. She looked thoughtful.

He quite carefully taped her neckline. He took his time and was artfully sure it was structurally sound with only two discreet pieces of tape. That took some study.

She stood still for it. He watched his hands on her chest, and felt the pulse in her throat. She watched his face, his eyelashes. When the time-consuming project was completed, he looked up into her eyes, smiled just a little, and gave her a fleeting kiss. Right there in his office! How shocking.

He told her, "I have been given the interesting privilege of telling you that you are being considered for the job of director of personnel here at Michaels Inc."

"I?"

"You."

"Why, how amazing!"

"Not at all. You've been doing the job for a long time. You might just as well be properly paid."

She looked at him suspiciously. "Does this announcement have anything to do with... with..." Her words ran out.

"Us?"

She nodded, quite appalled.

He went on. "No. This was an executive discussion between the local and expanded people. Your records are in all hands. At the meeting yesterday, we agreed to some changes. Your title and salary are one change. Michaels Inc. has used you poorly."

"Director."

He expanded it: "In line for VP."

"And our... We have nothing to do with this? You're sure?"

"I'm positive. I was tempted to tell you last night, but I thought it would spoil the evening. It would have seemed as if I'd wanted to use you. I didn't want this information to influence you."

"You thought I'd just . . . reward you?"

"No." He replied so seriously.

"But you thought I might think you would want me to be . . . grateful?"

"I didn't want the office to intrude into any of the evening. We might have gotten into a strategy discussion."

"I'm not sure I know how a VP walks."

"It's like putting on pants," he told her gravely. "You do it one leg at a time."

But she wasn't listening.

"If I'm director, what will you do?"

"I go back to headquarters, VP for marketing. I was here as a scout."

"You'll . . . leave."

"You knew I was here temporarily."

"Of course." She turned away.

"Sarah."

She didn't trust herself to face him. "Yes?"

"This weekend, could we go to Chicago together?"

"I'm taking my scout troop down to Turkey Run. We're using Joan's parents' cottage down there and it's for badges. Scout badges for their sashes—you know."

"I see. No substitute leaders?"

"Leaders are at rock bottom. I have three troops."

"And none of the kids even belong to you."

"I like kids."

He said, "There's something else. Phil is a crook. He's been stealing designs from this company. We're looking for him. If you should see him anywhere, let me know immediately. He contacted an honest company who alerted us."

She turned back then and looked at Steven. "He has nothing to do with designs. He's an accountant!"

"He's very clever. In a small organization like this, people feel free to talk about what they're doing. He listens."

"I hate crooks or traitors. I hope you catch him. What will they do to him?"

"We'll fire him. We just wonder how much harm he did the company. One of the feathers in Michaels Inc.'s cap that interested us is the research department. We bought your engineers."

"You bought the company for the engineers? Why didn't you just hire them away from us?"

"Well—" he laughed a little "—we did try. It seems they are loyal, they like working together, and they like Indianapolis. So the mountain came to Muhammad. And with an engineering bunch like that, that loyal, it was a shock to find a worm in the apple—Phil."

"I've never liked him."

"You're very sure you can't find someone else to take the troop this weekend?"

"My parents are going to go with me to help out. I'm the leader. I want to go. Want to come along? The girls would love you."

"How old are girl scouts?"

"Most ages, but these are thirteen."

"I pass."

"They're enchanting."

"So are you."

But he would leave. He was going to turn over the department to her, and he was going to leave.

Ted Zink, who was also a visiting marauder among the local female contingent, was jubilant that Phil Terry had proved to be a culprit. "How did you ever know?" he questioned Steven the next day in the hall. "No one else had a clue that he'd been pulling some hanky-panky. The books balanced. We hadn't a glimmer of suspicion. Was it the leave of absence?''

''I just had a hunch.''

''No wonder you're so good with people.'' Ted was admiring. ''It's like they say in the home office: No one knows people the way you do. You're a genius.''

''No, no, no, Ted. Don't make so much of it.'' How could he tell anyone the only reason for the inquiry was so he'd have an excuse to bring Sarah to the office on that first weekend? So he could see if she would be easy and thereby get rid of his shocking bemusement for her. She had turned out quite, quite differently. After he went back to the home office, he'd be concocting all kinds of reasons to check out Michaels Inc. in Indianapolis ... to see her again. ''Huh?'' His attention came back to Ted.

''I said, 'How soon do you intend to wind up this supervisory stay and get back home?' ''

''You miss Donna.'' Steven guessed.

''I didn't know I was going to miss her this much. You don't suppose I'm hooked at last?''

"You're young yet," Steven said bracingly. "Don't do anything stupid."

"All our buddies are falling by the wayside. Nowadays we're mostly buying baby gifts. As the last of the bachelors we're either going to go exclusive by desertion or recruit some younger friends."

"You're paranoid."

Ted shrugged. "I honestly think I'm caught. When I called her last night, her voice trembled."

"She was doing aerobics. You know women never do only one thing. They never just talk on the phone; they dust or put away the dishes or something. You probably just have spring fever. Take something for it. Go look at the steno pool. There's a world of women out there."

"Is this like AA?"

"Similar."

Nine

Throughout the day word spread that Sarah was to be the new personnel director. She smiled over the congratulations and exclamations, but she was oddly quiet. Everyone commented on how composed she was, with all the fuss, and that that was the reason she made such a good—she shuddered at the overused catchphrase—"people person."

Sarah was still in stock. Michaels Inc. was an old company, male oriented. They paid well enough, but ambitious women were ignored, and so women moved on to other companies. Sarah had given them no word of acceptance. She wasn't sure she wanted an executive position. She wasn't sure she wanted to stay in personnel. She didn't foresee any opportunity to marry. Although she'd only given up the last dregs of hope a month ago, she'd been using her crystal and silver for two years.

If she wasn't going to marry, her life was her own to do as she chose. There were a good many interesting things to do out there in the wide, wide world that didn't include a steady job with a guaranteed income. She wanted to explore the possibilities. How interesting that "possibles" included things other than eligible men. Interesting.

Possibles. She'd allowed her goal to be so narrow. Tunnel vision. She'd been so set on marrying that she'd wasted ten years in a mediocre job, doing her own plus the boss's work, and she'd never even looked at all the other "possibles" open for exploration. All the other experiences, all the other opportunities. How could she have limited herself!

It was almost five that Thursday when Steven asked, "Where shall we celebrate?"

"What?" She looked blank.

He laughed softly. "Still in shock?"

"About . . . what?"

"Being made director of personnel?" He grinned, very pleased for her.

"I haven't accepted."

It was his turn to go blank. He stared, astonished. "You have to decide?"

"Yes."

"We'll talk about it over dinner."

"No. It's something I need to think about."

"I'll help clarify issues."

"You're in marketing. You're a salesman. You're a charmer. A trickster. You'll sell me a bill of reasons that aren't mine just as an exercise in manipulation."

"I don't do that with friends. I am . . ."

"Say 'buster.'"

"I did it once but for good reason. I did that at the picnic so Phil wouldn't be able to harass you. I could have muscled him, but it could have become unpleasant. I might have lost! It was expedient to pretend to be drunk."

"And get me into bed."

He grinned. "A fringe benefit."

Very quietly she said, "I always wondered how a 'fringe benefit' felt."

"Now, Sarah! Just you hold it. You are off on a path that's full of thorns, and I'll be ripped apart following you."

She gave him a sober, very distant look and replied quietly, "Then don't follow."

"My God, Sarah..."

"They would like my decision tomorrow. I have to think about this. I'll see you in the morning." She was very formal.

He muttered something in a harsh, brief spat and turned away. And people said he could be manipulative. She had even said so. If he really was, she'd be going with him to his place. She would have been there this whole week. She was an obstinate, redheaded, trouble-maker! He was well rid of her.

Steven didn't call her that evening. He went to feed Lily Anna but she'd already been there. For her to have gone over to her apartment when Phil was out loose somewhere made him even angrier. Steven glanced at the singing cat and hated everybody in Indianapolis. He especially hated all the redheaded women who lived in that particular apartment.

She didn't know he didn't call. She had the bell off on the phone but the recorder was on. There were no messages. She ate some toast and tea because her stomach didn't really want anything at all, then took a deep, soaking bath while the dogs watched her with courteous interest. Afterward, she curled up on the bed to decide what she wanted to do.

However, it wasn't the position she considered. She thought about Steven Blake. She went over their entire acquaintance, and she realized he would leave her the way a sailor leaves port with his ship. She was only his Indianapolis Experience. His fringe benefit. How cheap.

After he left Indianapolis, she would never see him again—unless he came to Michaels Inc. or she had to go to the home office in Chicago. He would probably be perfectly willing to make love with her on any occasion. But what about her? What about what she wanted?

She had to face the fact that she loved him. She hadn't had an affair, casually and emotionally uninvolved; she had fallen in love with a man who was crafty and calculating. He didn't care one thing about her; he cared only about himself. He hadn't had a redheaded woman lately and she had red hair.

He was skilled. He knew exactly how to go about loving a woman. He must have been with dozens to make love so beautifully and sincerely. Any woman could be hoodwinked into thinking he meant it. It would be interesting to see how he would extricate himself from this affair.

Would he say she needed the opportunity to expand and experience this promotion so that she could fulfill herself? Or would he simply say he'd be in touch? Would he allow distance and time to solve the problem for him? That way would make it easy for him to break up with that redheaded greenhorn—what was her name?—down there in Indianapolis.

He might keep in touch for a while so he'd have a bedmate when he was forced to check out Michaels Inc. But what about her? Could she hang on for crumbs? Allow herself to become Steven Blake's convenience? Surely not. She must have enough backbone to show that she wouldn't be used that way. She'd refuse the promotion. Whom would she recommend in her place?

With a completely honest evaluation, she knew she would choose Bill Yost. Madeline Templer simply wasn't strong enough. It was very tempting to name a woman, but Madeline was the only woman who might be a possible for promotion, and she honestly could not handle every aspect of the job. She needed more training in organization, and she might never become positive enough to make decisions without wavering. That was depressing. Madeline would never understand. She was older than Bill and had been there longer.

How would Steve handle Madeline? Take her out to dinner and then to his bed? As far as Sarah knew, Steven had never given Madeline more than a cursory greeting. But then he was a sly man. He might very well be with Madeline right that minute... Was Steven really that way?

Whatever he thought of her, he'd been honest with her. He hadn't fooled her. He'd told her all along he'd be leaving.

And in her mind she was again skillfully kissed by him and once more felt his hands, so practiced, and knew his body, so marvelous. She knew she was bemused by a warlock, but she was strong enough to realize it and to fight his spells of mesmerizing her into his bed. She would not. Never again. Determined, she beat hell out of the pillows, then flopped restlessly around in the bed before she settled down and cried herself to sleep.

The next morning at the office Steven spoke to her very sweetly. She smiled at him just as if he were an ordinary person, and she was very, very, *very* busy all that morning. She fetched or corrected, or whatever, with great efficiency; then she hurried on her way to or back from her computer, or whatever he'd interrupted. She was as skilled as he, but she specialized in avoidance.

At two-thirty, she told Steven Blake that she would like a word with him, when he would be free. He gave her a careful look and said, "Now."

She sat across from him at his desk and told him, "I do appreciate the opportunity you gave me to be director. It was gratifying. For personal reasons, I am going to decline. If you..."

"You *decline*?"

"Yes. If you would..."

"Why?" He glowered at her.

She replied courteously but firmly, "For personal reasons." She said more firmly, "If you would like..."

"What personal reasons?"

She instructed, "Personal reasons are, of course, personal. If you would like me to..."

"What the hell kind of an answer is that? Here you'd be the first woman at Michaels Inc. to hold an executive position and you 'decline for personal reasons.' What kind of woman are you? A coward? You've been doing the bloody damned job all along, there's no reason not to have the title and the money. You give me one good reason why you're not taking this job."

Her blue eyes flashed splinters of warning. With a carefully pleasant voice she said yet again, "If you would like me to recommend someone in the department, I would..."

"I thought you were so business oriented, calm, cool and collected. A good male mind and attitude and you throw over this plum 'for personal reasons.' Either give me a good solid reason or I'll tear up your file and fire you."

"I quit."

"What?" he roared.

"I resign." She changed the word.

"What in the hell is the matter with you?"

"I refuse the position." She rose. "This is futile. I'll continue the conversation when you're in control."

He got up from his chair, shoving it back so that it crashed against the wall. Then he came around his desk so fast that she didn't have time to get away. She glared daggers at him, her mouth was tight, and she swung her body and thrashed her arms to get free of him.

He held her effortlessly, reached over and slammed the door, then grasped her upper arms in his hard hands. "You owe me some sort of explanation," he snarled.

Her eyes snapped with temper and she replied, enunciating exquisitely, "I owe you... nothing."

"What's happened to you? On Tuesday you were the sweetest woman I've ever known, and now you're a spitting cat. What in hell's happened? You redheaded rattlesnake! Do you think I gave you the director's position because you slept with me?"

"I don't want it. Let go of me. I'm no longer an employee. I've resigned."

"I may throttle you. How am I supposed to cope with a redheaded witch like you?"

"You don't have to. I am quitting and you'll be going back to Chicago."

He finally realized it wasn't just temper. She was serious. He eased his grip on her arms but still held her there. He was baffled. Everything was coming down around his ears. He said slowly, "Sarah, I don't understand."

"I've discovered 'possibles' also includes experiences. I'm going to explore the varieties of possibilities."

"And just what in hell does that mean?"

"I'm going to look for adventure."

"And you can't find it in the personnel department of Michaels Inc."

"I haven't yet. And I've given it ten years more than I should have. Do you need two weeks' notice? I'd like to leave today. Madeline is caught up on all my projects. I would be available in case of something staggering. But all my work is on schedule. We could pretend I broke a leg and Madeline would simply take over."

"You're serious."

"I've had a revelation. I know I want out of Michaels Inc. I want to be gone from here."

"This is frivolous. We almost had an undependable, frivolous woman as director of personnel. You have blackened the reputation of all women."

"Nonsense. This is not in the least frivolous! I'm trained, skilled, and I have solid job experience. How like a man to judge all women by one."

"Has your 'revelation' been precipitated by your relationship with me?"

"It was a contributing factor, but I had already reached the conclusion that I am not marriageable. I have no desire for a top-level job. I don't want to spend my life accumulating brownie points for Michaels Inc. I'm not a team woman. I want to fly free."

"You're too young to be going through the change. Is it your period?"

"Men have moods; women have periods. Why is it that all of mens' judgments of women hinge on their sex? That men have career moves but women have been dumped by a superior?"

"You feel I'll dump you?" He was shocked. "You're overreacting."

"Men react; women overreact."

"Sarah! I don't know what's hit you, but all of this is silly."

She corrected him. "The only thing silly in this confrontation is your reaction to my turning down the position and deciding to resign. It's perfectly simple. There's nothing complicated at all. I don't want the promotion, and I have decided quite logically that I don't want to continue here."

In something of an alien temper he snapped, "Why not?"

Coolly she replied, "I don't want to look down the years and see only this job. I want to work with children. I want to try something different. I want to test my wings. I want to live a more varied life."

"You're not old enough to have the middle-aged syndrome of discontent."

"Labels again. I want change, so it's my body chemistry. How about my hunger to experience another way of living? I'm grateful to you for offering me the position. Without it, I might have been another year or even two before coming to this decision. How or why I've turned this down and resigned is no one's business. It's none of yours either. I resent it that you've forced me to tell you so much. You have taken the news exactly as I expect a man to take such news from a woman; a man would be called adventuresome, but a woman is only considered flighty. Let go of my arms."

He stared at her. Then he said more quietly, "We need to talk."

"Some of the Blake manipulation?"

"Perhaps I only want to know you're all right; that you've really thought this out. And perhaps when I know what you want, I can help you to find it. I've run into all kinds of people who do all sorts of things. I may be able to put you in touch with someone who can help you find what you want."

"A psychiatrist." She gave him a very narrow stare.

"I've found a place for Joan down at the hospital through a woman I met in marketing. She's going to give Joan a job there that can be adjusted to Luke's schedule. They'll have more time together."

"Why, Steven, how nice of you!"

"If I know what you need, there's the chance I might know someone who would know how to help."

"Thank you."

"How can I help?"

She smiled. "I'm not sure. But when I figure that out, I will contact you."

"That's sounds distant."

"You'll be going back to Chicago..."

"It's not far."

"No."

The ignored phone began to ring yet again. He went to it saying to her, "Wait a minute," and into the phone he said, "Steven Blake."

But as he talked, she left the room. She sat down in her chair, drained. Her head had began to throb. She took a deep breath and took up her work where she'd left off. Her own phone rang. She lifted it and her father said, "Well, there you are. Where have you been?"

"Going mad."

"Oh. Is that all? I thought there might be trouble. I have good news and bad news. Your Aunt is better. But we can't be there for your fun trip to Turkey Run with your little scouts. Do you have someone to help you?"

Dismayed, Sarah replied, "Of course. No problem. Mom okay?"

"In her glory. You know her. All the kids have gained ten pounds on cookies alone. She's spring-cleaned the house and worked me to a standstill. I'll never be the same man again."

"Poor Papa."

"Well, I should have called sooner! That's the first sympathy I've had all week!"

"And you've gained ten pounds too."

"Well . . . she made those little crunchy ones that I especially like. She only allows the kids one at a time but I get three."

"And she lets you sleep late."

"Yeah, but then she won't let me nap. She's working my tail off."

"Poor Papa," she said again.

"We'll miss being with you and the girls. They remind me of you at that age."

"I was never that charming."

"No, but you were so earnest, and your red hair was so like your mother's. Because of you, I know what she was like as a little girl. And you're like her now."

"I was offered the position of director of personnel and the opportunity for VP down the line."

"Oh? And did you take it?"

"I've quit my job."

"Well, you're a long time coming to that."

"What do you mean!"

"It isn't your speed. You need something different."

"Well, Papa, you might have told me!"

"You never asked."

"What should I do now?"

"Take your savings and go around the world."

She laughed. "You're crazy."

"Oh, yes. Your mother's told me that for years. I believe she told me that the first time..."

"When you went into the library and there she was, with a shaft of sunlight on her hair, stamping books."

"Oh. Have I told you that before?"

"I'm going to miss you two this weekend."

"Let us know all the jokes they tell."

"I will." Sarah said goodbye to her dad and hung up. She would miss them. Now, who on earth could she get to go along? She looked up as Joan walked by and she smiled.

"Whatever it is," Joan said to her, "the answer is no."

"You'd miss the opportunity of a lifetime."

"Oh-oh. This is a serious hit. Now what do I want in exchange for whatever it is you're... Ah-hah! This is the girl-scout weekender. You have my folks' place in Turkey Run, your folks are with your aunt and you're...uh-hmm. Let's see. You know that green silk gown I covet? It looks tacky with your red hair but it goes with my eyes. Okay? And you get Luke to fix up any cuts or abrasions. We get the whole attic to ourselves. Okay?"

"I'll give you two times with the dress. And with Luke's medical services guaranteed, I'll give you an option on the spangly one next Halloween."

"In writing."

"I won't sign in blood."

"Red ink will do."

"Done." Sarah held out her hand. "Nice doing business with you."

Joan shook her hand. "Steven has fixed me up to work at the hospital."

"Are you pleased?"

"I'm irritated I didn't think of such a simple solution."

"Can't see the forest for the trees." Sarah nodded sagely. "With his offer for me to be director here, I've quit my job."

"I'm not sure I see that as a solution to your life. You're being a lot more pragmatic than I."

"I'm not executive material."

"Hah! It's what you've been doing these long years. Taylor got the money and you did the work."

"I was glad for something to occupy the time."

"I wish I had a company so I could hire you and work you into the ground and pay you a pittance. I'd make a bundle."

"My dad suggested I use my savings and go around the world."

"And . . . Steven?" Joan's voice was suddenly soft with concern.

"He always said it was temporary here."

"And you?" Joan watched her with seeming casualness, but her eyes narrowed against her friend's hurt.

"It's been interesting."

"Who'll be director?"

"I've recommended Bill. Madeline needs a little seasoning. I wish I could honestly recommend her now."

"I believe she'll understand. When she heard you'd been offered the job she said, 'I'm glad I'm not the one.' So don't worry about it."

"I would be guilty of reverse prejudice if I nominated her over Bill."

"Quit sweating it!"

"Right. Thank God you'll go this weekend."

"Two times with the green and the spangly for Halloween."

"And Luke takes care of all cuts and abrasions. He'll be swamped by 'injured' scouts. He looks so romantic with his dark eyes, sunken cheeks and beard."

Joan smiled falsely. "I'll be there, right by his elbow, and I'll pinch those giggling girls if they get fresh with Luke."

"Polly recalls that quite vividly."

"We'll meet you in the morning. You can handle it alone tonight. Okay?"

"Good enough." Sarah smiled fondly at Joan. "Thanks."

* * *

After Joan left, Sarah sought Madeline and asked, "Could you take over for me this afternoon? I've my troop for the weekend and it would help if I could get a start on it—check out the food and pack the car. I've got one station wagon borrowed, and one of the fathers is driving down another load tonight. Could you take over?"

"Sure. And I hope you take the job as director. You've been doing it anyway."

"Your time will come," Sarah said evasively.

"Not for a while. I'll let you get the job broken in and then I'll try it."

So that afternoon when Steven came into the office and found Madeline at Sarah's desk, he asked, "What's going on?"

Madeline replied, "She left you a note. She has her troop at the Parkington place down at Turkey Run this weekend and she took this afternoon off to get braced for it. If I were Sarah, I think I'd have spent the day in a bar. I went with her once and it took me a week to recover. She handles it as if it's fun! Strange woman. Oh, and Phil Terry called, so I told him where she was. He's on leave from Michaels Inc. I don't believe you've met him. I asked if he wanted to talk to you, but he wanted Sarah."

Steven's hair stood on end. "Where is the Parkington place?"

"Joan will know."

Steven's sense of danger was intense. In his mind's eye, he saw the broken window in Sarah's bedroom and her clothes strewn around. Sarah would be down there in the woods with all those hysterical little scouts and she'd have no warning. Anything could happen.

Ten

Sarah's note to Steven read, "Please don't forget to feed Lily Anna." That was all. No name. No *o*s or *x*es for hugs and kisses. Just not to forget to feed that damned, drunken cat. He called both her house and her parents' and left the message on their answering machines: "Phil Terry knows where you'll be. Call me."

Then he asked Madeline to feed Lily Anna that weekend. She wasn't thrilled; she already knew the rum-soaked cat, but she understood and agreed to do it.

While he waited, he asked Madeline to call Joan into his office. He was afraid to leave the room or use his phone in case he'd miss a call from Sarah. When Joan came in he explained the situation and asked for a map to her parents' cottage. "I'm going down there. I've a call in for her, but she apparently isn't home or she's ignoring my message."

"Phil won't harm her. He's always had a yearning for Sarah. I believe it's her hair. Some men become peculiar around redheaded women."

"Really?" He contrived to appear surprised.

"Yeah. Strange."

"And green-eyed brunettes?"

She smiled a marvelously smug smile. "Want to follow us in the morning? We're going down about ten and get there after the brats have had breakfast."

"I'll go tonight."

"It's a little tricky in the dark."

"I'll find her." Steven sounded very sure of himself.

Joan contemplated him as she considered the fact that he hadn't said he would find the place, or the troop or the area; he had said he would find *her*. Did he realize yet that he loved her? Did he know Sarah loved him? Nothing else could have triggered Sarah's desperate decision to quit her job in order to escape except the thought that Steven would never marry her. She believed that he'd simply leave her with a fond pat; and she was too smart to be an occasional companion or a live-in love. Any woman recognized that for a proven disaster. So Sarah was disordering her life to remove herself from temptation. While that was smart for self-preservation in a hopeless case, it now appeared that Steven loved her. Joan smiled. How interesting this weekend would be!

Sarah's errands took the rest of the afternoon. She didn't go by her own apartment because Lily Anna would be all right. Steven wouldn't fail him. And in passing—in the rush of getting organized—she did note that the message light on her parents' recorder was on but who knew she was there? Her parents knew she would be in Turkey Run, the office could get along until Monday, and she just didn't have time for chitchat. So she didn't play the tape.

She gathered her share of the scouts. They drove south from Indianapolis, into the hill country, then on down to the Parkingtons' cabin. Supper was part of badge time, with various cooking duties done with chewed tongues and frowns, burns, and the usual teasing, gagging and hilarity. Sarah was in her glory. The scouts added *r*s to her name: Sarrah, or several *r*s for Sar-r-r-rah. It seemed as if someone wanted her attention every second.

With permission and scout care, they built a fire in a metal lid to sit around in the cooling evening, and sang. They were loud and roisterous in their high-decibel talk, but their singing voices were soft and feminine. They charmed Sarah.

Phil did arrive. His car drove up and, for just a heart-stopping instant, Sarah thought it might be Steven—she had invited him—but it was Phil. He was subdued. He came to the fire, uncertain of his welcome. The girls giggled and rustled as they moved. Phil was a good-looking man, and they were so curious!

"What are you doing here?" Remembering the trashed room, Sarah stood up, her hands on her hips as she faced him with her back to the fire. She was intensely aware of feeling very responsible for the young girls in her care as she concentrated on remembering her judo.

Phil didn't know if Sarah had written the letter terminating his employment at Michaels Inc. He'd received the certified-letter notice in his box, and had to go to the post office and sign a return receipt in order to see the letter. He'd thought it was a reply to his offer, but it was from Michaels Inc. They knew. Someone in the company he'd contacted had reported his offer. It was ironic that he'd probably contacted the only honest man left in the world. Did Sarah know?

"I just came around to tell you goodbye. My uncle and I are going abroad."

"Goodbye."

Not a good beginning. He smiled at the gaggle of young girls. "Do you still sing 'Waiting for Our Chow'?"

They laughed in a ripple of giggling amusement. They were friendly anyway.

He inquired, "May I join you for a while?"

He was so different. Sarah watched him and realized that he knew Michaels Inc. was on to him. Her heartbeat picked up. What was he capable of doing? Was he dangerous? All those parents had allowed their children to go—with just her. No one else had the time. Only she could give these scouts this outing. And there she was, alone, with a man who had broken a window and tossed her things all over the room in a fit of temper. A man who had betrayed his company.

What was she to do? Keep the kids together. Did he have a weapon? She would attack and yell for the kids to scatter! They'd practiced scattering for search and find. They could do that. She was poised and keyed.

He sat cross-legged, affable, smiling at the girls who covered their mouths to laugh and whisper, their eyes dancing, their movements quick and a little excited by Phil's presence.

Sarah remembered all the mass murders. All those who didn't believe it could happen and waited as they did nothing. She could *not* let anything happen to these precious girls. She stood there and said, "Gingerbread! Scatter."

Everyone over nine knows "gingerbread" is the secret word for danger. It's the only word that contains all the letters for danger.

There was the least hesitation, then the girls disappeared in a rush. Phil half rose, searched the empty area and looked at Sarah blankly. He asked quickly, "Gingerbread? Danger? Where? What's gong on?"

"What do you want here?" Sarah asked.

He stood facing her. He questioned: "Sarah? You think *I'm* the danger?" Phil looked appalled.

"My room." She stepped back and said only that and quite coldly.

He turned his head. "What is it? What room? Sarah, what's going on?"

"My broken window, my clothes all over everywhere. Nothing missing."

"What in *hell* are you talking about?"

"I wouldn't expect you to admit it."

"Admit *what*? Honest to God I've not one

clue! Are you in danger here? Has someone been in the cabin? Do you have a gun?''

''Would I tell you if I did?''

''Let's get the kids into the cars and go for help.''

''No. They will be hidden until you leave.''

''Sarah, for God's sake! I'm no danger to you. I came to see if you will go with me. Just as friends. I've such a . . . case on you. I know you're not at all interested, but I've heard you quit your job and you told someone you'd like to travel. I'm going on a tour. Come with me.''

''Why are you here?''

''I was afraid if I didn't catch you this weekend you'd be gone before anyone knew it; I'd never find you again.''

''You didn't trash my room?''

''Here at Meyers'?''

''At my apartment.''

''Why in hell would I do a stupid thing like that? I'm trying to make you like me. Do you think I'd do something that dumb and scare you off?''

''Who did?''

''How would I know?''

Then Steven arrived. The car swung in by Phil's and Steven was out of the car and running toward the pair standing by the fire. "Sarah!"

"Steven?"

"Sarah!" He grabbed her arms in the same old hold and set her aside as he confronted Phil. "What are you doing here?" It wasn't a question but a territorial demand.

Phil became bristly. "What about you? You're hardly a girl scout."

"You get to Sarah only through me!" Steven was leaning forward, snarling, extremely aggressive, and more than a touch belligerent. His arms were up, his fists clenched and he jabbed his thumb in his own chest to indicate who was talking.

When they looked back on it it was really exciting. At the time it was unbelievable and irritating—and everything went out of control. Sarah was the only calm one in that maelstrom of suddenly visible scouts who were squealing and yelling and jumping around. Phil took a swing at Steven and Steven loved it.

Sarah was trying to restore order and no one paid any attention to her at all. She got mad.

With Phil on the ground and Steven looming over him, urging him to get up, Sarah hung on Steven's arm, shrill and getting hoarse. She found herself saying, "Watch your language!" That seemed odd to her. Then she said, "I want this stopped *this instant*! You scouts settle down. Back up. Who allowed you free from 'scatter'? You all get demerits for disobedience. And what sort of role models are you two for *scouts*? How shocking of you! Get up, Phil. Shake hands, you two."

Steven smiled. "Yeah, get up."

Phil wouldn't.

It ended up in a shouting match between Sarah and Steven, her rescuer. She stood in front of Phil with both hands pushing on Steven's chest, her red hair like a flag for a bull, her eyes shooting fiery blue sparks as she and the bull yelled at each other. Phil prudently stayed on the ground, while the scouts stood around, grinning, hugging themselves in the excitement of witnessing this unexpected adult conduct, knowing Sarah had two men fighting over her.

It was interesting that both debaters knew all about Phil's piracy, but even in their tempered exchange over Phil, neither mentioned it.

With outrageous confidence, Sarah turned and braced her back against Steven's chest and held out her arms as she said to Phil, "Go now. Good luck." Behind her ear she could hear Steven's excited breathing and her back could feel his heat, his aliveness—his power.

Phil eyed Steven distrustfully and began to rise. Steven shifted enough so that both Phil and Sarah knew he could have moved anytime in any way. It was only his self-control—in obedience to Sarah—that was preserving Phil.

Even then Phil said, "Go with me, Sarah."

"Good luck," was all she replied.

He turned and walked away in silence. The scouts were awed by the whole episode. It had been just, well...wow! And there were those of the observers who felt a sympathy for the defeated man.

Phil reached his car unchallenged, got into it and started the motor to back up slowly. His car's headlights swept around as he turned and drove away amid the silence of a group who knew it had all been deliciously dramatic. Steven growled in Sarah's ear and she remained standing in the harbor of his body with her back against his chest. Still dangerously on the prowl, he asked, "Why didn't you let me throw him out?" This from a man who was a professional friend.

With a supreme confidence in her ridiculously puny strength, she slowly turned her head to look up into his bent-down face and replied, "You're jealous."

"No. Why should I be jealous of a little weasel like him?"

"I haven't the foggiest."

"Why would you be so nice to the little insect?"

"He didn't know anything about the room. If it wasn't Phil, who in the world could have done that?" She became aware, with their calmer speech, that they had an avid audience. She began to straighten away from Steven, but he put his hands on her arms in the same old lock and held her there. She said, "The children," in a very quiet voice.

He jerked up his head and looked at fifteen pairs of entranced eyes. He grinned and said, "Well, hello. What were you doing just standing around? Why weren't you helping me? A great bunch of scouts you are!"

He won them over, just like that. Then he settled in to stay. And he adroitly captured all their hearts. A clever, manipulative man. Sarah said with a snub, "This is for ladies only. You cannot stay."

"I'm quite good with girls," he replied.

She uttered a quelling "Yes, that's obvious."

"I have sisters. I can even braid hair." He looked down his nose at her with great superiority and his devoted audience laughed in appreciation. And to enslave them further, he added *rs* to Sarah's name. They loved it.

None of the scouts wanted to go to bed that night. Steven handled it. He said no one could get to them past him, they were safe. They giggled. He said, "How can I court Sar-r-r-rah if you all are listening?" That did it. They hustled into the cottage, into their sleeping bags, and lay in complete silence, straining to hear.

So he had her alone by the dying fire. They'd been so noisy earlier that there weren't any of the night sounds. He tidied the fire as he whistled contentedly through his teeth. He settled down beside her, crowding her a little. She shifted as if she were making room, but she didn't move away. He said, "So you plan to go around the world."

"I won't even ask how you know that."

"I'm omnipotent."

"Yea, lord."

"Good attitude." He watched her as she watched the fire. "So you've given up on finding a suitable man?" He waited for her nod. "You've implied you might settle for having children. I wouldn't mind giving you children."

"Ah, but would you be there for birthdays and holidays?" Her heart picked up its beat.

"I would *have* to show up on occasion to be sure you weren't in the mood for another baby. Just to check up, you know. See how many were around, and how many more you'd need."

"Ah, so generous."

"Would it be all right if I stayed in between times? I would like to sit and look at you holding our babies."

She had to open her mouth a little so that she could breathe. "How are you at spiders and mice?"

"I can handle mice. I'm terrific at mice."

"What about spiders?"

"Well . . . I really don't like spiders. I had a fake one that I put in the girls' beds and loved their screeches and all. However, one night they dangled a humongous rubber spider over me as they shone a flashlight on it that made it look really gruesome. The experience marked me at that impressionable age, so I've been a little leery of spiders since then. Surely if I took on the mice, you could handle the spiders?"

"I would have to weigh that negative against any other positives."

"I'd be great in bed."

"Statistically, women should marry younger men. Your sex drive would probably fizzle."

She raised her brows as she invited his rebuttal.

"Fizzle? What a terrible word!" he protested indignantly. "I'll have you know the men in my family outlast three or four wives. We all start late and last forever. My grandfather had to get married when he was ninety-two." He gave her the dregs of indignation slowly being replaced by a polite look. He mentioned, "A mania for redheads runs in my family. I inherited this obsession from my dad."

"What did you get from your mother? Does she have any obsessions?"

"She likes men, but I didn't get that gene, I inherited my dad's."

"I see. It's nice you took after your father."

"Yes. But there's the problem of introducing you to him. We're going to have to go about this carefully. He's a prime case. I haven't it as badly, I know, because I fell in love with you in the parking lot and you had on a hat that covered your hair. You didn't take it off until we were inside, in the hall, and I almost gave up when I saw your hair. Because of my dad, you understand. He has high blood pressure and redheads tend to disturb his count.''

''Are you sure you want to become involved with me? I know you like making love with me, but you were not nice to me at first . . .''

''That was strictly self-preservation.''

''And you told me this was temporary. You did say that just yesterday.''

''I was still struggling against you.''

''Why?''

''You want me to say it.''

She smiled. A laughing smile.

''Pretty confident, aren't you. Did you know all along?''

''Only when you came here like a knight in shining armor. You were magnificent!''

''Why didn't you let me squash him?''

''He was squashed enough.''

''He wanted you.''

''So did you.''

''But I got you.''

''Yes.''

''Tell me you love me.''

She raised her eyes to his and said it so serenely. "I love you."

Cockily he inquired, "Are you sitting worshipfully at my feet?"

"Surely not."

"I believe you are."

"Men are only meal tickets," she scoffed.

He added, "And women, just warm bodies in a bed."

"If you expect me to warm your bed, you'll have to marry me."

He grinned. "I did suspect that."

"What do you mean?"

"At first I thought there was the chance you'd fall into my arms without any preliminaries. You were so confident and friendly. But you didn't even try for me! You didn't even smooth your hair when I took you out to the office that first time. You weren't in the least susceptible to me. You've taken a hell of a lot of work," he complained.

"You're very deliberate and manipulative. How will I know when you're sincere?"

"I'll be my own grouchy self, and you'll have to cosset and soothe me and think of ways to make me happy. Want the job? I'll give you a home and children. As big a home as you want, and all the children you desire. That is what you want, isn't it?"

"And a man who loves me—sensibly."

"Sensibly? Is this in the fine print? Why sensibly?"

"I don't want a man who will fall against the wall when I come into the room. I want him able to handle being in love with me."

"I love you, Sarah. Sensibly." He reached over and took that same grip on her arms as he turned her and drew her across his chest. And finally he kissed her. There in that faint glow of the dying fire, out in the woods in southern Indiana, with fifteen scouts straining to hear what was going on, he kissed her breathless, making her toes curl and her hands clench him and her body press against his.

They sat like that most of the night. He held her there, smiling. His hands moved on her back, and he took kisses now and then with great contentment. How strange he could hold her, need her, and not have to take her. He said, "That first time we made love, I thought

I took you in passion, but even then it was love.''

She made sounds in her throat. ''When did you know?'' It was the time for exchanges of why and when and how; of all their feelings for each other; with impossible declarations. Strange talk between a woman who has given up on marriage and a man who is a confirmed bachelor. They murmured there in the night and their laughter was soft.

They spent that weekend in a haze. They smiled into each other's eyes, they touched, they noticed when Luke and Joan came, and they were polite to their hosts. The scouts laughed and giggled and followed the mesmerized pair, who walked side by side not touching, but so glued by just their glances that they could have been locked in each other's arms.

It wasn't until late Sunday that they delivered the last of the scouts to their homes. Then they went on to Sarah's apartment to make love and lie in bed with plans and talk and laughter.

There was no further threat to Sarah, and they never found out who had broken the window, entered her room and thrown her clothes around. The police speculated it may have been a wrong address.

Sarah's family took to Steven reasonably. Her father relinquished her with some nostalgia and sympathy for his own wife's father all those years before. Her sister accepted him as another male in a very male household and went her busy way.

Steven's family was another story. He couldn't risk taking Sarah to meet his folks. So he let them meet over the phone and he told his mother the problem, "Sarah's a gorgeous redhead."

His mother replied in sympathy, "Oh dear."

Leaving Jim Blake in Chicago, Esther met her daughters in Indianapolis to judge the hazard Sarah represented. They viewed her soberly and pronounced, "Disaster," and exchanged worried looks.

Sarah emphatically pronounced, "I'll dye it."

Esther protested, "No! We'll put our minds to this. If we can work it, he'll be so proud of you."

* * *

They sent pictures of Sarah to Mr. Blake—gradually clearer, more focused ones—until he became desensitized to her, as Steven explained it to Sarah, "About the way one does with shots to desensitize against rattlesnake venom."

She huffed a while before she could sputter, "You're comparing me to *rattlesnake poison*?"

He agreed. "You're about that lethal. I've had a fatal dose of you."

"Awww. Show me where it hurts."

With Steven's father finally able to cope, Steven and Sarah were married that September. Mrs. Thompson's gift to them was Lily Anna.

Six years later they had four children—twin sons and two daughters. The eldest, a girl, was named Joan Ann but the kids had nicknamed her Jo Nan.

"Another one?" Steven asked as they lay in their giant bed early one morning after they had been invaded and surrounded by their little ones. "This has got to stop."

"Why?" Sarah inquired with a tumbled look as she kept the one-year-old from toppling off the side.

"I could have a hard time finding you," he complained.

The kids hooted laughter at their dad not being able to find their mother when she was right there, and even the three-year-olds gurgled deliciously and joined in pointing out their mother with little, star-shaped hands.

"One more." Sarah smiled at her husband.

In spite of being surrounded with children, he looked like an untamed pirate with his morning beard and tousled hair. He sighed long-sufferingly and grouched, "If that's what you are dead set on, then I'll have to conserve my strength."

"Breakfast in bed?" she guessed.

He grinned at her, but there was a noisy clamor among their offspring as they scooted to the head of the very large bed, turned and leaned back against the piled pillows yelling, "Me too, me too!"

She exchanged a smile with her lover, then rose from their bed and stood in her sea-green gown with her back to him as she stretched. She was a glorious thirty-five by then, and he a magnificent thirty-nine. They had not reached the peak of their potential.

Leisurely she shook out her cloud of red hair and twisted it up in an attractive, careless mass to pin it it on top of her head. Then she went gracefully to the bed and, with slow deliberation, leaned one hand on it for support as her toes guided themselves into her slippers.

It had been several years since Steven had last taped a gown's neckline to her chest and she looked up in time to catch his slitted eyes on her décolleté. She smiled wickedly, and his replying rumble was marvelous. With their children around, she could be quite bold in her mannerly tempting.

She straightened and made a flirtatious tease of her walk to the chair that held her black, gold-embroidered Chinese jacket. Then she slowly put it on, knowing how he watched and turning her face over her shoulder to see that he did, then she smiled at him quite smugly before she left the room and went down the stairs.

In the kitchen was the comfortable woman who cooked for them. They greeted each other in affectionate voices and Sarah said, "Breakfast in bed."

Mrs. Franklin sighed. "Finger food. You change the bed and vacuum or Mary Katherine will have a fit," she admonished.

Sarah agreed to that and added with a smile. "And bananas." She sliced six of them into a bowl. Then she added a seventh for the new little Possible.

* * * * *